Forbidd
(Double Love MFM Romance)

By

Terry Towers

Forbidden Indulgences

Cover By: Melody Simmons

http://ebookindiecovers.com/premade-ebook-covers-erotica/

Copyright 2014 by Terry Towers

This book is a work of fiction. Any resemblance to persons, living or dead, or places, events or locales is purely coincidental. The

Prologue

~ 15 months ago ~

Ivy

"I can do this. I can do this," Ivy Sullivan repeated over and over as she stared at herself in her bedroom mirror.

She was so nervous that her stomach was churning and she was frightened she might be sick. Although there wasn't much in her stomach to unload, she'd been so nervous that she hadn't been able to eat all day. But it was nerves, that's all. Once she told her stepbrother how she felt and it was out there everything would be okay. He'd tell her he loved her back and then they could move on as a couple. Sure, the whole stepsibling thing would cause some issues, but their parents had only been married a few years, certainly not long enough for her to consider him as a *real* sibling, more like a roommate. She'd played the scene out in her head a million times over the past month and it never ended badly.

But years of insecurity and a lack of confidence were fierce opponents, wanting her to remain in her room, shut the door and continue to pretend she was okay with just being his friend. But that was a lie and she couldn't live with a lie any longer.

At least I'm heading to college tomorrow, she mused, *if he doesn't feel the same I don't have to see him again. Or at least not for a while.*

She gave her appearance another once-over. She'd spent close to an hour getting ready, making sure her makeup was flawless and her auburn hair shining without a strand out of place. She'd searched every store in Portland, Maine looking for the perfect dress. While the one she selected wasn't perfect it did a pretty good job at flattering her body shape.

She normally wore sweatshirts and oversized t-shirts in an attempt to hide her chubbiness, but it never really helped. However, this dress was cute, it actually made her look like she had a waist, accenting her figure in all the right places. Having been a girl who'd struggled with a weight problem her entire life, usually weighing anywhere from 80 to 120 pounds more than her "ideal" weight, feeling beautiful and desirable was oftentimes challenging. However, this was one of the first times in her life she felt beautiful, she felt like she might actually have a chance with the captain of the football team who had stolen her heart without knowing it and slept across the hall.

Just maybe…

Taking a deep breath in, she slowly released it and gave her appearance a nod. It was now or never. She left her room and crossed the hall. There was the faint sound of music coming from Ethan's room – *Linkin Park*. It was a band he loved and always played when he was in an especially good mood.

He was in a good mood, that was a bonus.

Ivy knocked on his door, waited a minute and then opened it up, peeking her head inside. "Hey Ethan, you busy?"

Ethan looked up from his laptop in her direction, while muting the sound, then spun his desk chair around and gave her a smile. "Not really, what's up?" He was gorgeous, everything about him was perfect in her mind. Everything from the way his blue eyes shone when he laughed to the way he could make her feel good just being around him. He wasn't just a random guy she had a crush on, but one of the closest friends she had and if he rejected her it would ruin everything.

And it would crush me, she silently added.

She opened the door fully and stepped inside, closing it behind her. The last thing she wanted was someone – namely one of their parents – overhearing what she had to say.

"Wow, you look amazing," Ethan stated, letting out a low whistle. "Big plans for your last night here?"

A blush warmed her cheeks. "No. No, I wanted to talk to you though." She crinkled her nose at him. "It's kinda important."

He motioned toward the bed. "Have a seat. Let's talk. What's on your mind?" He sat back in the chair he was sitting in and laced his fingers behind his head. "You know I'm going to really miss having you around to hang out with."

Ivy graced him with a smile. That was an encouraging statement.

"I have something to say and I'm just going to say it, okay?"

Ethan frowned, leaning forward in his chair and eyeing her a little more critically. "Ummm. All right. You can tell me anything, you know that." He took her shaky hands in his and gave her a smile of reassurance. "Come on. What's up?"

Just do it. Just do it. Like a Band-Aid. One rip and right off!

"I love you Ethan," she blurted, not able to look him in the eye as she said it.

Seconds passed, maybe minutes. She couldn't say for sure, it felt like an eternity. When she couldn't stand the wait any longer she looked up into his eyes, which harboured a mixture of confusion and disbelief.

"Ethan?"

He slowly pulled his hands from hers and straightened in his chair. "I don't understand." His eyes focused on a spot above her left shoulder. Then down at the floor between their feet. And then down at an imaginary piece of lint on his t-shirt. He looked everywhere but at her. In the million scenarios she'd envisioned, this wasn't how any of them went down. The fact he'd pulled his hands from hers also did not seem to be in her favor.

"I love you. I'm in love with you, Ethan. For quite a while now to be honest." She looked up at him, hopeful. He just needed time to digest the information. He hadn't turned her down yet, there was still hope.

He stood abruptly, sending his chair tumbling backwards, and thrust a hand into his hair. He didn't seem to notice the chair was now on its side. "I don't understand what you're expecting me to say, Ivy." He began pacing, back and forth. "What am I supposed to say?"

She chewed at her lower lip and shrugged. "You love me too?"

He stopped pacing and stood before her. "I do."

Her heart soared.

"As a friend. And my stepsister."

Her heart went crashing into her stomach. "But…"

"I've never considered you in that way, Ivy."

"I just…"

He gave his head a little shake, catching her gaze for the first time since she'd made her declaration. "I'm sorry, Ivy."

A sob caught in her throat and tears filled her eyes. She leapt from the bed and brushed past him. When he grabbed for her hand she shook him off, racing from his bedroom across the hall and into the sanctuary of her own room. As soon as the door to her room was closed and locked she allowed the tears and sobs free rein. She began practically tearing the crimson-coloured dress from her body and tossing it into the corner in a heap, not giving a damn it cost her three weeks' pay working at the local coffee shop as a barista. She'd never wear it again so what would it matter.

As she lay curled up in a ball on her bed she hoped Ethan would change his mind and come to her, telling her he messed up and wanted her too. He didn't. She left the next morning without saying another word to him.

Chapter 1

~ The Present ~

Ivy

"I can't believe it, Ivy. I just... Wow."

Ivy caught her best friend Cassidy Reynolds' blue eyes in the full-length mirror on the back of her closet door and smiled. She refocused her attention to her reflection, and her smile widened looking at the beautiful green-eyed girl staring back at her. "One hundred and twenty pounds," she said, more to herself than Cassidy. It wasn't until she arrived home and saw all the pictures of herself at two hundred and forty pounds that how much weight she'd lost really hit home; she could barely believe she used to be that girl.

"One-hundred and twenty pounds. That's how much I weigh now. Amazing, huh?"

"It's insane. It really is," Cassidy confirmed.

It was. All her life she was always the fat girl. Throughout school she was always the "fat friend" who stood by and watched all her friends go out on dates and have boyfriends while she stayed home on the weekends hoping she could be one of those girls, the beautiful ones, like her stunning blonde bombshell best friend Cassidy.

Middle school had been a nightmare, she'd been teased relentlessly – high school was marginally better. It still hurt when she gave it any thought – so she didn't. At least she tried not to anyhow.

"I think we need to go out and show you around. Fifteen months away from home is way too long to go without my bestie."

Ivy was tempted, but she was on a mission tonight. She turned to face her friend. "I'm really sorry Cassidy, I really am. I just… after what happened… I needed to get away and then when I started losing weight I didn't want to come back until I was the new me…" she crinkled up her nose, tossing her auburn hair over her shoulder. "Does that make sense?"

Cassidy got up from Ivy's double bed and walked over to give her friend a warm embrace. "I get it. But I just don't understand why you'd even want him after he was such a jackass to you. He doesn't deserve you. He didn't then and certainly doesn't now."

"I want him *because* he was such a jackass," Ivy corrected. Her mind rushed back to the memory of her spilling her heart out to her stepbrother before she left for college. His rejection was swift and perhaps a little blunter than he'd intended, but he'd made it clear, she wasn't his "type." Meaning, she was a little too chunky – correction, too fat, to warrant his interest. No doubt it was her weight because up until that moment they'd been close friends, their personalities matching perfectly. Her yen to his yang. Her confession and his rejection changed all that.

"Do you think this looks good on me?" Ivy ran her hands along the red form-fitting mini-dress she was wearing. The dress clung to her curves like a second skin. She wasn't used to this type of clothing and still felt a little ill at ease showing off her body. So many years of insecurities about her body had taken a toll on her self-esteem, she supposed. She'd always admired the larger girls who seemed to own it, she was just never able to.

"It's incredible. You're easily the hottest woman in town, he'll be drooling over you and I guarantee he'll be kicking himself for being such a jerk before. So what's the plan anyhow?"

"I'm going to seduce Trey."

Cassidy's brow knit as she took a step back. "I don't get it. It's Ethan you want. Why?"

A wicked smile spread across her lips. "Because I'm going to have them both."

"Excuse me?" Her friend's blue eyes widened in surprise. "What do you mean?"

"I mean. The best way to get at Ethan is to go after his best friend. Besides, you know how badly Trey treated women in high school. He deserves to be taught a lesson just as much as Ethan. Think of all the girls they've cheated on and left heartbroken over the years. It's about time someone showed them how bad it feels to be treated like they're insignificant."

"But how? I mean…" Cassidy raked a hand through her golden hair. "You know they're both a couple of playboys – that hasn't changed since you've been away."

"True, but here's the thing. They both expect the women to fall head over heels like they always do for them. They don't expect to be the ones being led on. And they always go for looks, not what's in the woman's head."

"Yeah, but how do you expect to rope them in? I mean you're gorgeous… But…"

"Because, I know them. I know them both, extremely well. I know how to catch them and how to reel them in. I know what they like in a woman, and I know how to be that woman. I know my weight was the only thing holding Ethan back before. Without that between us it should be easy enough."

Despite her words she was still nervous. Well over a year had passed. They might be entirely different people by now. According to Cassidy they weren't, they were the same kind of guys who'd left her broken-hearted, but there was no guarantee.

Cassidy draped her arm over her friend's shoulders. "Well, on the behalf of half the women of Portland, Maine, if you can pull this off, we thank you. About time those jerks learned a lesson."

~*~*~*~*~

Ivy's heart rate accelerated as she heard the roar of the two Kawasaki Ninja motorcycles coming down the street and then rolling into the driveway of their parents' two-story home. Ethan had moved out last year, but was housesitting while their parents were on vacation travelling by train across Europe.

Maybe this is a bad idea. She looked at herself in the full-length foyer mirror. Nervous green eyes stared back. The thought that within a couple of minutes she'd be face to face with the guy who broke her heart was bringing back all the feelings of insecurity she'd felt before the weight loss.

"I'm not that girl anymore," she coached herself, nervously patting down the front of her dress, smoothing out any wrinkles. She had a week before their parents came back to accomplish her plan. Once they were back she doubted she'd have the opportunity to get both Ethan and Trey together – alone. Ethan would be back living at his place and she'd have failed her mission.

The motors of the bikes shut off and she sprang into action, rushing to the kitchen fridge waiting for the moment to open, bend over, displaying her bottom, while she pretended to look for something inside. She smiled to herself; despite her nervousness she could barely wait to see the look of shock on their faces. The few people she'd seen in town who had known her before she left didn't even recognize her now.

~*~*~*~*~

Ethan

"After last week, it's good to have a few days off to relax." Ethan placed his motorcycle helmet on the table next to the door and rolled his shoulders. He was severely cramped up. With one of the worst heat waves in history baking Portland, the amount of forest and field fires that had taken place over the past week had also been at a record high, keeping him, Trey and the rest of the men at the fire station insanely busy and pushing them past their limits of exhaustion with all the overtime they'd had to put in.

"Yeah. Two weeks without a day off fucking sucked," Trey agreed, placing his helmet next to Ethan's. "I need a beer, don't suppose your folks have…"

"Yeah, I stocked up the other day."

"Maybe we should head to the clubs tonight. It's been a while. I could use some serious stress relief."

Ethan's hand shot out, stopping Trey from proceeding around the corner and into the kitchen. He placed his index finger against his lips. Trey frowned, but nodded his understanding. He heard movement coming from the kitchen. Suspecting it was an intruder he motioned for Trey to cover his back as he slowly and silently rounded the corner and peered into the kitchen. His eyes immediately caught sight of a slender woman with her back to him, bent over and rummaging through his parent's fridge. The short dress she was wearing had pulled up and was an inch from revealing her in her entirety to him.

What in the hell is going on? I'm sure I locked the door this morning. Even better question who in the hell breaks into someone's house and raids their fridge? Crazy people, that's who.

"Excuse me. Miss…" He cautiously advanced on the woman, not sure what to think of the female intruder, but not taking any chances considering she may be some crazy woman. Trey was hot on his heels as the woman straightened up, a bottle of water in her hand and spun around, her long auburn hair whipping into her face as she turned. She raked her fingers through her hair, pushing it back out of her face and his heart stopped a moment.

"Ivy?"

He could barely believe his eyes. If it hadn't been for her emerald green eyes and how her lips curled up into a wide smile of greeting he wouldn't have recognized her.

A wave of guilt washed over him as his mind flashed back to the day before she left for college. She'd told him she was in love with him and he'd rejected her. That was the last time they'd spoken. He tried calling her numerous times over the past year, but she refused to answer any of his calls or text messages; she wouldn't even come home from college for the holidays. They'd been so close before that moment and went from being good friends to strangers, and the guilt tugged at him knowing he was to blame for it.

"Well, hello Ethan." She looked past him and smiled at Trey. "Trey. So nice to see you again."

"Wow. Ivy, you look… Smoking." Trey stepped up from behind him and walked over to Ivy.

Her green eyes lit up at the compliment. "Thank you Trey. It was hard work, but this is the new me."

"I *love* the new you," Trey responded with a wide smile spreading across his face.

Placing her bottle of water on the counter, Ivy slid her arms around Trey's neck and hugged tight to him. Ethan's jaw clenched and a surge of jealousy raced through him as he watched his best friend and Ivy embrace. Trey lifted her off her feet and she squealed with delight.

Ivy remained extremely close to Trey even after the hug ended and he placed her back onto her feet.

"Geez man!" Trey motioned toward Ivy. "Don't you think you should pay little step-sis a compliment?" Trey's eyes moved up and down the length of Ivy's body. "She's turned into a goddess."

"I would have if you'd have given me a second, jackass." Ethan attempted to simmer his temper. Trey didn't have to make him look like a douche. "You look really good, Ivy. I'm really glad to see you again." He stepped up to her and gave her a hug, but she was tense in his arms, not hugging him with the enthusiasm that she had Trey.

I get it, she's still pissed. He sighed as he separated from her.

As soon as she separated from him, she turned back to Trey, virtually ignoring him. "So Trey, I hear you're both firefighters now."

"Yeah, yeah. It's been *a long* couple weeks. Lots of fires."

"I bet." Ivy's green eyes remained on Trey's dark ones, ignoring Ethan. "So Trey, any new girlfriends?"

"Nah. Not for a while. Ethan and I are both having a bit of a dry spell."

Thanks a lot man. I'm an asshole and having a dry spell, you're making me look more appealing by the second. As soon as the thought came to mind he frowned. He'd made his choice over a year ago. He'd told her he wasn't interested, so it's not like it mattered anyhow. Over a year of her ignoring his numerous calls said everything he needed to know. But dammit, she could have at least given him an opportunity to explain, to apologize, to smooth things over. But nothing. As soon as he said he couldn't return her feelings she'd taken off and locked herself into her room, refusing to talk to him. And that had been it; the end of their friendship and dammit he'd missed her.

"Listen Ethan, I know since I'm here now you really don't have to, but I was hoping since mom and your dad are away for the week you could hang out at the house with me. It's quiet and so empty, compared to the dorms, ya know?" She turned to Trey and added, "Both of you really. We could catch up." She gave Trey a side hug.

Anger and jealousy surged through Ethan again. Not cool.

"Yeah, I guess. I'd still need to drop in each day to check on your mother's parrot anyhow. Pepper is on a special medication and needs to be hand fed the medicine anyhow. And, well, you two don't seem to have the greatest of relationships. Do they even know you came home?"

"Yeah. They've known a while. And for the record that parrot had it out for me from the moment Mom brought it home. Nasty bird."

Ethan's frown deepened. "They didn't tell me."

"I told them not to."

"Why?" As soon as he asked the question he growled at himself. He didn't want Trey privy to what went down between them. He shared virtually everything with Trey, but her professing her love for him was the one thing he'd kept to himself. "Never mind," he grumbled under his breath, cutting off her chance to answer.

Ethan looked at his friend, wanting to ask Trey to leave so he could talk to her in private. But what good would it do? She may be mad but at the same time maybe it was his overactive imagination, maybe he was the one still fucked up over what happened. Hell, looking as she was now, he imagined she had every frat boy on campus falling over himself to be with her. She was the package: a wonderful person, too smart for her own good and now drop-dead gorgeous to boot. There's a good chance she was over him now and if he were to even bring up the idea of them together, she'd be the one rejecting him and he'd look foolish and conceited for thinking she carried a flame for him.

"I was thinking that I could make us all some supper. Maybe we could all spend the evening catching up?" Ivy walked back over to Trey and gave him another quick side hug.

Three hugs in less than ten minutes, seriously, what the fuck! Ethan seethed, then growled at himself for the foolishness of his emotions.

"What do you say? I've learned some amazing recipes. Low fat and delicious! And it looks like there's a case of beer chilling in the fridge."

A wide smile spread across Trey's lips and he nodded. "That would sure beat the pizza we were planning on ordering."

"So, yes?" Her expression turned hopeful as she looked from Trey to Ethan and back again.

"Yeah." Trey nodded to Ethan. "How can we pass up an offer like that, huh?"

Ethan's eyes narrowed at Ivy. She had never taken this much interest in Trey before and she hated beer so he suspected she had planned this out already. What was her game? She'd never been like the girls they went to high school with, she wasn't one to play games. Had that changed as she lost the weight? That would be such a damned shame, she had so much to offer a man she didn't need to play games. Or it could just be his ego running wild again.

If she had so much to offer then why did you turn her down? a voice at the back of his mind chimed in. He had no answer for that question, only guilt and regret. His mind quickly went back to the question: What was her game plan?

Now she has a game plan? Man, get over yourself. Chances are she's well over you, his conscience argued with him.

"Yeah, that sounds wonderful," Ethan confirmed, a little more dryly than intended.

Chapter 2

Ivy

Despite it being over a year and her transformation, just seeing Ethan again sent Ivy's emotions whirling. The hurt, the fear, the attraction and even the love came rushing back. He'd always been well-built, but he appeared to have gained even more muscle. He'd matured into a man even more attractive than he'd been, although she'd never have guessed it possible. She hated him for it, but hated herself even more for how much she still wanted him; how much she wanted him to want her...

But he doesn't, she silently reminded herself as she pulled the pan of chicken breast from the oven and set it on top. *Nothing has changed.*

"Need any help?"

Ivy froze as she heard Ethan's voice behind her. Closing her eyes she slowly counted to five before reopening them, pasting a smile on her face and turning to face him. "If you don't mind grabbing a strainer and getting the pasta ready that would be great. The sauce is done and waiting in the saucepan."

She turned back to the cupboard, reached up and pulled down three plates. To her dismay her hands shook ever so slightly. *I'm not that girl anymore.*

Ethan stepped up beside her with the pot of spaghetti and gave her a little hip bump. "I got this, if you can grab some beer from the fridge and set the table." She attempted to worm her way back to the spot she'd once been, but he gave her another nudge with his hip.

"Stop it!" Laughing, she bumped him back. "Bully."

He chuckled. "Your part here is done, little sis. Now go get that beer. And I'm not a bully, you're just in the way."

Looking up, Ivy's eyes caught his rich blue ones. For a brief second, time rewound to before she proclaimed her love to him and they were friends again goofing around while preparing supper. During that moment, she contemplated dropping the whole thing and settling for just having her friend back again. The thought was a fleeting one.

"What's a guy gotta do to get some food around here?" Trey asked, walking into the kitchen. "Something smells delicious."

Ivy pulled her gaze from Ethan's and looked over her shoulder at Trey. "As a matter of fact it's done." Turning away from Ethan, Ivy walked over to the fridge and grabbed three bottles of beer, opened them and set them onto the table as the men plated up the food and set it onto the round four-person oak table. Normally she'd steer clear of alcohol, but she decided to make an exception for the week.

The men sat down with Ivy between them.

"So what's this sauce?" Trey asked, swallowing the first bite of whole wheat spaghetti. "It's amazing."

"It's a secret," Ivy replied, giving him a wink. "And it's low fat."

"And what's a guy got to do to find out that little secret?"

Ivy's eyes locked to Trey's and she saw something there. It wasn't simply friendship like it always had been. There was a definite interest. While she'd thought she'd felt a spark with Ethan before she went away to college, this was the first time she'd ever felt any type of spark with Trey. But then again they weren't as close as she had been with Ethan. *See Ivy, there you go. He didn't have any interest at all when you were Ethan's fat stepsister, but all of a sudden now that you're thin he's flirting with you. Coincidence? Doubtful.*

"That's a secret as well." A saucy smirk spread across her lips.

Trey groaned, rolling his eyes at her before thrusting another forkful of spaghetti into his mouth.

"How is school going, Ivy?"

Ivy turned her attention back to Ethan. "Good."

He raised a brow at her, clearly wanting her to elaborate.

"It's challenging. Much harder than I expected to be honest."

"But you're doing well?" He stopped eating and focused all of his attention on her. She shifted uneasily in her seat. She'd already had this conversation with their parents, she had no desire to have it with Ethan too. She'd been so focused on creating the "new her" that her studies had fallen to the wayside.

"I've had a lot on my plate. Going away to college is so much different than high school. With so much going on at campus, sometimes it gets hard to focus."

"But you graduated with high honours, Ivy. You're fucking smart and study hard, you're on a scholarship for shit's sake, you should be breezing through."

Ivy stabbed at the spaghetti with her fork and twirled the pasta on her plate, her face flushing slightly. "I still study hard, but maybe not as much as I should."

"Why?"

Ivy frowned, anger bubbling to the surface. "Jesus Ethan, you sound like Mom. Lay off. So I like having a social life for a change. Maybe it's nice to actually get to go out on dates and have guys interested in me."

"So it's a guy. You're going to let some asshole screw up your future?" His eyes were burrowing into her. If she didn't know better she'd have thought she saw a flash of jealousy in his blue eyes.

"God, Ethan, you're like a dog with a bone!" She cringed as she heard her voice rising with each word. This wasn't at all going the way she wanted it to go. "I'm just supposed to remain a virgin the rest of my life? Maybe instead of going to college I should have joined a convent and not bothered working my ass off to lose all the weight I did."

"I expect you to respect yourself more than to go 'girls gone wild' at some university and throw your future away." Their gazes locked, neither one willing to break. Ivy gritted her teeth; how dare he!

Trey clearing his throat uneasily pulled Ivy's gaze from Ethan's and she looked back down at her plate, thankful for the diversion. "I think maybe you're overreacting a bit, man. Ivy's always had her shit together; I doubt she's throwing her future away. Just chill."

Looking over at Trey, Ivy shot him a smile of gratitude. She never expected Trey to swoop in and rally for her. "Thank you Trey. I'm just getting my footing." She shot a look at Ethan. "That's all."

Reaching over to her, Trey placed a hand on her leg, just below the hem of her dress, and gave her leg a little squeeze. Catching her lower lip between her teeth she tried to ignore the heat that formed under his hand and crept up her leg to ignite the need within her. There was no mistaking it now, there was definite chemistry with Trey.

~*~*~*~*~

Ethan

Ethan gritted his teeth as he looked over at Ivy and then Trey as they shared a look. He knew the look Trey was giving her, knew it all too well, and it was pissing him off. Trey had no right to look at her like that. He'd never had an interest in Ivy before. Her future was important, dammit. Maybe Trey didn't give a shit, but she wasn't *his* stepsister.

Stabbing at the chicken he thrust a piece into his mouth and chewed fiercely, not really tasting the food, but attempting to pull his thoughts from the idea of Trey and Ivy together. The idea of the two of them naked, together, limbs entwined, Ivy moaning his Trey's name flashed into his mind. It was driving him near insanity.

The thing was that it wasn't so much the fact that he didn't want Trey with Ivy, but it was the fact that *he* was the one Ivy was supposed to want. But instead, she was arguing with him and giving Trey the sweet sexy smile that was supposed to be for him. *Him* dammit!

Grabbing his half-empty beer he downed the remainder. *Let it go man, let it go. You had your shot. ...* He couldn't.

"So instead of studying so you can be a doctor, like you've dreamed of being, you're wasting it... For what, to get laid by some frat boy?" Pushing his chair back, he stood and made his way to the refrigerator and grabbed another beer. When he spun back around he was face to face with Trey.

"What the hell is wrong with you man?" Trey whispered. "You've been worked up this past year because Ivy took off without a word to you and now that she's back you're being a fucking dick. Give her a damned break."

Taking a deep breath in, Ethan slowly exhaled as he twisted off the top of the fresh bottle of beer. "You don't get it Trey and I don't feel like explaining it. She's not your responsibility."

"And she's not yours either. What I get is she cooked us dinner and asked us to hang out with her for the first time in over a year and you're going to chase her off. What the hell man?"

"You don't get it," Ethan repeated. He looked over Trey's shoulder to see Ivy, who was picking at the barely touched food on her plate, and another surge of guilt rushed over him. Trey was right, he was being a dick. She was here and he was finally going to have an opportunity to explain why he'd rejected her and he was close to blowing that chance – for what? His ego? Because she may be interested in someone other than him? "It's complicated."

"Well, you have a choice, stop being an ass or I'm taking her out of here for the night. It's not cool, man."

"Fine." Ethan attempted to move past Trey, to be stopped. Their gazes locked. "I said, it's fine." Giving Trey a shove out of the way,

Ethan stepped past him, walked across the kitchen and took his seat to the right of Ivy. "Ivy, I'm sorry."

She looked up from her plate and stared at him a moment. Brushing a lock of long auburn hair from her face she nodded and lowered her gaze back to her plate. "No big deal."

~*~*~*~

Ivy

"So are you seeing anyone now, Ivy?" Trey asked.

Ivy's head whipped around to gaze back at Trey, a smile returning to her lips, grateful for the distraction. Taking a deep breath in she slowly released it, building her courage. "Not right now. I've been dating but no one has really caught my attention for very long. So what about you two, you said you've been having a bit of a dry spell?" She looked from one face to the other.

Trey shrugged. "It seems like this city is much smaller than it was when we were in high school. There doesn't seem to be much in the way of quality dating material left."

Maybe 'cause you two went through so many in high school, she mused, but merely smiled. "Now that seems awfully hard to believe. You guys had your choice of girls before I left."

"Maybe we're not the guys we used to be," Ethan cut in.

Looking back at Ethan, Ivy's eyes narrowed at him. "What do you mean by that?"

"We're not in high school anymore, Ivy. We had our fun times, but I'm sure I speak for Trey as well as myself when I say we now realize there's things more important than just looks and popularity and all those silly things that meant so much when we were teenagers."

"Those things seemed rather important to you a year and a half ago, Ethan."

Ethan sat back in his chair and crossed his arms over his chest. "People change, Ivy." He motioned toward her. "It's evident that you changed, so why can't we?"

Their eyes locked, but neither one spoke. She had a million thoughts racing through her head, second-guessing her plot.

"Well, that was a wonderful supper, Ivy." The sound of Trey's chair being pushed back broke into her thoughts and she pulled her gaze from Ethan's to look up at Trey. "How about we go on into the living room and maybe throw on a movie or something? A comedy perhaps." Trey's eyes cut over to Ethan's. "I think this conversation is over." He cocked a brow up at his friend. "Don't you?"

Chapter 3

<u>Ivy</u>

"Beer anyone?" Ivy placed the beer on the coffee table in front of Ethan and Trey. This was their fourth while she nursed her first wine cooler. Just how she'd planned it. The awkwardness of the confrontation at the dinner table had seemed to die off as the night wore on and for that she was grateful. She needed them to be at just the right state that they'd be in a carefree mood and up for just about anything, but not so drunk they'd be useless. They were almost there. The idea wasn't to go for the gold tonight, but plant the idea in their heads, let them simmer on it overnight – maybe for a few days.

"Yeah, I'm about due for another, babes," Trey said. He guzzled down the remainder of the beer in the bottle, placed it on the coffee table with the other empty bottles and accepted the fresh one from her. Ivy turned from Trey to offer to hand one to Ethan and yelped as his hand landed on her bottom with a playful smack. The slap left a sting in its wake.

"Trey!" Turning back to him, Ivy gave his shoulder a swat. "Keep that up and I'll have to cut you off."

"Oh, you don't want to be doing that Ivy." Placing his beer on the side table, Trey grabbed her hips and pulled her back and into his lap.

Ivy squealed as she fell back onto him and wiggled on his lap as she attempted to settle herself on him. As she wiggled, she felt his shaft thickening beneath the layers of clothing and the ridge of his cock pressing against her bottom. Her body froze for a brief moment, surprised by his body's immediate reaction to her, despite that being the intent from the beginning. He'd certainly been sending her signals, but it was still a little startling. She'd dated some at college, but was still getting used to men's reactions to the new her.

She was about to spring from his lap, but one look up and into Ethan's jealous eyes reaffirmed her need to see this through. She was getting to him, making him feel how she'd felt the day he'd turned her away. Instead of squirming away, Ivy sank back into Trey's embrace. As she leaned closer a whiff of his cologne drifted to her nose, a woodsy scent with citrus undertones; it was enticing, inviting her closer. It felt both awkward and incredibly good being in Trey's arms.

Redirecting her attention from Ethan to Trey, she grazed her lips along the side of his neck, pretending to inhale his scent. "Mmmm. I love your cologne." His body tensed under her, his hands tightening their grip on her hips and he groaned softly, although not loud enough for Ethan to hear.

"Thanks. I'm glad you like it." She pulled back and their eyes locked. Desire had flared up within his dark eyes and she could see the fight to restrain himself in his expression.

"Oh, I do," Ivy purred and nearly cringed at the way she cooed at him. She was reminding herself of those slutty cheerleaders she hated so much in high school. No matter how much hurt Ethan caused her and they caused other women, did she really want to stoop to being just like those girls? Because the bottom line, even though she hated to admit it, was that she still wanted Ethan and she was beginning to have feelings toward Trey, even though the ones for Trey were mostly based on attraction. But he seemed to have changed. Maybe they both had.

Is this what I really want? Maybe this was just a plain bad idea.

Ivy looked down into Trey's dark lust-filled eyes and then quickly glanced over at Ethan, whose blue eyes were filling with rage. Was she over her head? *Better question, who was I to think I could ever pull this off?*

Ethan

What. The. Fuck!

Ethan was hitting his breaking point watching Ivy with Trey. He was trying to ignore it, but neither one of them seemed to be shy about their excessive flirting, while he was virtually ignored. It had been going on for hours, through dinner and two movies. There wasn't enough liquor in the fucking world to calm him at this point.

To hell with this! When Trey nuzzled her neck and she closed her eyes giggling he'd had enough. Slamming his empty beer bottle down on the coffee table Ethan stood and stormed from the living room, heading up the staircase to the bedrooms. He wasn't sure what he was angrier about: the fact she was being so open to Trey's advances or the fact it was bothering him as much as it was.

What did it matter anyhow? I had my chance and I rejected her.

He didn't even want to consider the guilt. It had been eating at him since she took off to college. He'd been an ass and he knew it. He'd rejected her because of what… 'Cause she was fat and he wanted the beauty queen on his arm. She was the perfect woman and he'd given her up and now it appeared she was going to be Trey's. If he could turn back time and have a redo on that moment when she'd told him she loved him he would in a heartbeat.

Maybe I don't deserve her anyhow…

Reaching the top of the staircase, he made his way to the room that had been his until a year ago and entered, slamming the door behind him. Remembering that he had a pint of Jack Daniel's tucked away on the top shelf of his closet from his high school days, he grabbed it and then flopped himself onto his bed intent on getting himself nice and hammered to override the feelings swelling and swirling within him.

Fine, let Trey have her. It's not like she'd want me after what happened. She'd made that crystal clear, and it fucking hurt.

Ivy

Seeing Ethan storm off didn't give Ivy the satisfaction she thought it would – quite the opposite, it left her feeling guilty and ashamed.

"What the fuck was wrong with him?" Trey asked, all playfulness gone as she pushed herself off of his lap and onto the sofa next to him.

"I don't know." But she was lying, she suspected she knew. Looking up and into Trey's eyes she came to the conclusion that Ethan must not have shared that she'd bared her soul to him, which was unusual since they knew virtually everything about each other – talking about women and conquests had always been one of their favourite topics.

Why didn't he tell Trey? Maybe he was embarrassed... of me... for me. She frowned looking toward the staircase. She didn't know which. She had to find out.

"Are you okay? I was just messing around."

The sound of his voice pulled her gaze from where Ethan exited back to Trey. She forced a smile on her face. "Of course I am. I know."

"It's just..." he shrugged. "You've really transformed into a stunning woman, Ivy. It's hard to keep in my mind who you were."

She huffed. *Yeah, fat Ivy. The girl who had a beautiful face, too bad she's so fat.* She'd overheard one of Ethan's other friends say that more than once. She'd run to her room and cried for ten minutes and then found relief in a bottle of Coca-Cola, along with some chips and dip. They had been her friends and vices – still would be had she not replaced them with exercise.

"Damn." Trey thrust a hand into his short dark hair. "I think I'm making this worse."

Ivy's green eyes caught his dark ones. "No. It's good." She looked over her shoulder at the staircase outside of the room again and then back at him. "It's good. We're good." Sliding from the sofa she stood and adjusted her skirt, which had risen dangerously high on her thighs. "Just give me a second to see if everything is good with Ethan, okay?" She hesitated and with a surge of brazenness she leaned down and brushed her lips across his, kissing him softly, but pulling away before he could deepen the kiss; if that happened, she'd never get upstairs to get to the bottom of things, she'd be putty in Trey's hands.

Standing, she readjusted her skirt once more and gave him another smile before spinning around and rushing up the stairs. She had to move quickly or she'd lose the nerve – or before he got so much alcohol in him that he'd be impossible to reason with. If she recalled correctly he had quite a stash of liquor hidden in his closet and seemed intent on getting wasted tonight, so just because he was heading upstairs didn't mean the drinking was ending anytime soon. While a drunk Trey was flirty and fun, a drunk Ethan was not even close to being a fun person to be around.

Approaching his door, she paused with her hand on the door handle. It was in his room where she'd opened her heart to him to have it handed to her on a platter.

"That was a lifetime ago," she murmured, opening the door and stepping inside.

"Ever hear of knocking, Ivy?" Ivy's eyes lifted to see Ethan. He'd removed his shirt and was reclining against the head of the bed in a pair of black jogging pants with the Bangor FD emblem on the thigh. There was a long scar on his side that hadn't been there before.

She shrugged. "It's something I'll have to work on. Can I come in?"

"Looks to me you're already in." His eyes scanned her, slowly, from head to toe and back again. He didn't even attempt to hide his examination, or the look of annoyance on his face.

"Can we talk?" She took a few more steps into the room and closed the door behind her, not wanting Trey to hear their conversation.

He took a swig from the bottle of Jack and then set it onto the night table by the bed. "Why now, Ivy?" He sat up straighter on the bed and slid his legs over the edge, leaning forward and bracing his elbows on his knees. "Do you know how many times I tried to call you after you left? You wouldn't even give me five minutes to explain."

All right, guess we're going there already.

"What was there to explain, Ethan? I told you I was in love with you and you didn't want me." To her surprise tears sprang to her eyes. How could this hurt so much when it was so long ago? She turned slightly, enough so that he wouldn't notice her swipe at her eyes with the back of her hand.

"That wasn't it exactly."

"So you rejected me because of what? I was too *hot* for you. Too smart. Too good of a friend? Too devoted. Loved you too much. Come on Ethan, stop me when I've come to the reason!"

He frowned, his stare catching hers. "We're stepsiblings, Ivy… We were living under the same roof."

She huffed. "So my weight had nothing to do with it."

He opened his mouth to respond.

"Don't lie to me."

He snapped his mouth shut again.

"Yeah." She gave her head a shake. "That's what I thought. I wasn't the tiny cheerleader you could show off. I get it."

Ethan rose to his feet and all of a sudden seemed taller, larger. And too damned sexy. He took a few steps toward her, but she held her ground. Ivy tilted her head up, keeping her eyes locked to his, refusing to back down.

"Maybe you're right to a certain extent. A year and a half can make a big difference in someone – as you know. So maybe back then I was a bit of an ass and was swayed by the popular girls and women like that. But people change, Ivy. When you left and refused to talk to me it really hurt."

A laugh escaped her. "Hurt? You were hurt? You have got to be kidding me right now. You were given a choice and you didn't choose me and now you what… You want what? Pity from me 'cause you lost your fat friend?"

"I never saw you as that."

"But you never saw me as someone you'd want to be with either."

"I never saw you as someone to be with because you were a good friend. And we're stepsiblings. And let's not forget the fact you told me a day before you left for college. Just out of the blue, just before you leave you announce you were in love with me. Even if I had felt the same way, how did you figure that would play out? Me here and you in Boston?"

"We could have made it work, Ethan. It's not like I was across the country. It's not like Boston is very far. You just had to hop in a car and drive south an hour and a half."

"But you didn't give me time to process it, Ivy. You tossed it at me and then took off. I tried to talk to you, but you shut me out."

"If you really wanted to sort it out you could have come after me." She knew she was beginning to become unreasonable and that what he was saying did have some merit, that there was a chance her weight wasn't the only thing that had been a factor, but didn't give a damn. She needed a reason to pursue her plan. The plan had been the outlet for her heartache for a long time.

"So drive down there, while in the middle of training for the department so you could slam the door in my face and tell me to go fuck myself? If you wouldn't answer the phone no matter how many calls or texts I sent what would lead me to believe showing up and making a fool out of myself in person would provide better results?"

She frowned. She didn't have a reasonable answer for him. "You could have tried."

"And what is going on with you and Trey? You never had an interest in him before. At least I didn't think so. What's your game plan, Ivy? You're using him to make me jealous? Is that it?"

Ivy chewed at her lower lip, averting her gaze. The truth was that she didn't really know anymore. A few hours in the guy's presence and her whole plan was falling to pieces at her feet. There was a definite attraction toward Trey and it rivalled her attraction to Ethan. It was surprising and confusing at the same time.

Ethan sighed, drawing her attention back to him. She stared up at him as he thrust a hand into his brown hair in agitation. "Don't answer that, Ivy. I don't want to know."

"But –"

His gaze shifted to meet hers. "Can we just forget that past happened and just start over? Maybe just accept my apology and go from there. I handled the situation wrong and I don't think I'm entirely to blame, but if accepting full blame can help put this behind us then I'll happily accept it."

She hesitated for a brief moment, but eventually nodded. "I'd like that."

"Good." He took another step closer, then two, pulling her into his arms. This time she didn't tense or hold back like she'd done in the kitchen, but fell into him, slipping her arms around his neck and burying her face into the crook between his neck and shoulder.

Unlike Trey who had the enticing smell of cologne Ethan was simpler and more natural, soap and aftershave. It was equally good and enticing and seemed to reflect their personalities. Trey had always been the wilder one, he always tended to do things in a big way. Ethan had always been the quieter and more responsible one. The only thing the two friends had in common was the fact they were devilishly handsome and sinfully sexy in their own unique ways and they were desired by most of the women Ivy knew.

He pulled her tighter and she responded. "That's more like it."

"Huh?"

Ethan chuckled. "The hug. You're actually hugging me like you mean it and not like I have some disease or something."

"I didn't –"

"You did. And it's okay. Maybe I deserved it." He pulled back from her and she immediately missed the feel of his body against hers. It had felt so damned right in his arms. "I'm not feeling great. I think it's a mixture of exhaustion and too much alcohol. I'm going to hit the sack, but I'm sure Trey will be happy to keep you entertained."

"All right. 'Night." She grabbed the doorknob and went to open the bedroom door when he stopped her, his hand over hers. She looked up with questions in her eyes and met his gaze.

"We're not the same men we were, Ivy. Neither of us are. And yes, we did know you had a weight problem, but we never considered you the fat girl, even if that's what you may have felt."

Chapter 4

Trey

Trey watched her in amusement from atop his bike as Ivy eyed his motorcycle with skepticism.

"I don't think this is what Ethan meant when he said you should entertain me today while he's working. Personally, I was thinking we could drive down to the beach," Ivy stated.

"We will." He patted the back of his bike with his gloved hand. "But on this, not in your car. It's too nice of a day to be cramped up in a car."

Ivy looked down at the helmet in her hands then back up at him. She looked so damned cute in the leather jacket and tight jeans it was becoming agony to keep his hands to himself. The memory of their kiss the previous night kept replaying itself in his mind and he wanted more. The problem was that her demeanor had changed after she'd come back downstairs from her talk with Ethan; she'd gone from flirty and seemingly into him to subdued. He wasn't sure quite yet what that meant – neither she nor Ethan said what they'd spoken about – but he intended to find out. Usually he preferred working the same shifts as Ethan, but was glad this week their shifts were alternating so he could get some alone time with Ivy.

"But, I've never been on the back of a bike before. What if I do something wrong and the bike falls over or something?"

A wide grin spread across Trey's lips as he looked over his shoulder and patted the back of his motorcycle seat again. "Get on, hold tight to me and that's all you need to do. Come on. The girl I used to know wouldn't think twice about it. Has college made you uptight and rigid?"

"That's a nervy assumption."

He shrugged, his smile widening.

Cocking her head to the side she returned his grin. "Fine. You win." Pulling a pair of black leather gloves onto her hands she swung her leg over the bike and settled in behind him. "Uptight my ass." Pressing her front tight to his back she pulled the full-faced black helmet over her head.

"Tighter." Grabbing her hands in his, Trey pulled her even tighter to him, until she was flush against him and then settled her hands around his chest. "Ready?"

"Yes."

~*~*~*~

Ivy

He started the bike and it roared to life. Her legs tightened to the machine under her as the vibrations of the bike between her legs raced through her body. Excitement filled her. Despite her slight fear of being on a bike she'd always secretly hoped Ethan would take her for a ride, but he never did.

The bike lunged forward and she yelped, tightening her grip around him and placing her forehead against his shoulder. Hearing him chuckling, she smiled as they pulled out onto the street and tore down it.

While she was initially timid, after Trey took several turns with expert ease she began to get used to the feel of the bike under her. Her confidence in Trey increased and she was able to relax somewhat and begin to enjoy the ride. In fact, there seemed to be something soothing and sexy about being behind Trey, cuddled tight with the roar of the motorcycle engine in her ears and bike vibrations rushing through her. Twenty minutes later, when they pulled into the parking lot of the nearly deserted beach, she was disappointed the ride was ending so soon.

Slipping the bike into a slot, Trey cut the engine and kicked the kickstand down. With reluctance, Ivy released her tight grip on him and swung her leg out, sliding off of the bike. By the time she finished fiddling with the chin strap of the helmet Trey had already removed his gloves, helmet and jacket and was leaning against the bike, arms folded across his chest watching her with amusement dancing in his dark eyes.

"You could have helped, you know." She hung the helmet off of the handle of the bike, bent over and fluffed out her hair. When she straightened back up her eyes met his; the amusement had disappeared and was replaced with hunger. It took her by surprise and for a moment her breath caught in her throat as their eyes locked.

"Come here a minute." Trey crooked his finger at her.

Ivy's brow furrowed as she took a step toward him, then another. "What's wrong?" She raked her fingers through her hair, trying to straighten out the flattened mess the helmet had made of it. "My hair –"

Once she got within his reach he grabbed the front of her leather jacket and pulled her to him until only a couple of inches remained between them. "Your hair is fine." His gaze lowered from hers to settle on her lips.

She looked down at the ground between them as she ran her tongue along her lower lip. "Then –"

Releasing her jacket, Trey cupped her chin in his hand and forced her face up so she was looking him in the eye. His lips turned into a sexy smirk and sent her pulse racing. "You owe me something."

She crinkled her nose up at him. "I do?"

"Yup. And I think I've waited long enough." Before she could respond his lips were on hers and the hand that was grasping her chin slid around to the back of her neck, urging her closer to him.

Every nerve ending in her body seemed to come alive at the feel of his lips on hers and the need to be closer, for even more intimate contact became undeniable – and why shouldn't she? There was no harm in wanting him. Sure the point was for him to want her, but there's no reason why she couldn't enjoy the ride, she just couldn't get emotionally attached – that's all. As their tongues duelled, she fisted the front of his shirt, attempting to keep her desires in check. But the feel of his growing erection against her stomach and his hands sliding down her back to grasp her ass, pulling her tight to his erection was fuelling her desire, coaxing her body to respond in turn.

Unclenching her fists, she placed her palms flat against his chest and pulled away; another minute of his teasing tongue and roaming hands would surely be her undoing. She pulled away gasping, her face flushed and her heart thumping so quickly in her chest she feared it may break through her rib cage.

Trey

The girl could kiss, no doubt on that. Trey had been disappointed when the kiss ended, but seeing her rattled with her face flushed was both amusing and sexy as hell. She was a refreshing mixture of sexy and innocent. He'd always enjoyed Ivy's company and he'd secretly admit that in the past he may have overlooked her as a partner. In the past he'd had a tendency to go after girls who were assertive in what they wanted and had no problem making their intentions toward him clear. Ivy on the other hand had always been so shy and reserved – her self-consciousness clear. But now, the Ivy standing before him held onto many of the characteristics he liked when they were friends, but she'd grown such confidence. She shined both inside and out.

He had no idea what had gone on between her and Ethan, but it was evident something had. He suspected he knew, he wasn't blind, he'd taken notice of how she looked at him before she went off to college, but chose to keep his mouth shut on the matter. If either of them wanted him to know what had gone on, they'd fill him in. But with his interest, shouldn't he find out? At least a crib notes version.

"Ready to go for a walk?" He didn't wait for a response, but took her hand in his and began to lead her through the parking lot and to the beach area.

"I'd forgotten how nice it was here."

Trey scanned the small beach and nodded. "Yeah, it's incredible at sunset." He regretted bringing her in the afternoon and not a little later.

"It's not that long until sunset." They were halfway to the water when Ivy stopped and pointed to the deserted playground. "Over there." Giving his hand a tug she led took the lead as they made their way to the playground.

"I told myself I wasn't going to ask this question, but I think I need to."

She looked up at him and frowned, but continued walking.

"Are you? Do you? With Ethan?"

Her frown disappeared and a smile spread across her lips and she laughed. "Are we, do we, what? Come on and spit it out, I don't remember you ever getting tongue-tied before."

Trey placed a hand on the back of his neck and gave it a quick squeeze attempting to loosen the knot forming in the back of his neck. This was awkward, but the last thing he wanted to do was step on Ethan's toes; it's not like they could slice her in two and each have a half.

"Do you have a thing for Ethan? Before you went away I suspected maybe you did, but…"

She spun around and pointed toward the slide. "Come on, slide with me." He followed her to the slide and climbed the stairs after her to the platform.

"I think we're a little big for this, Ivy."

She smiled, looking at him over her shoulder. "Yeah, but there's no one here to rat us out so I think it's okay." Sitting on the platform, she gave herself a push and squealed as she slid down and jumped to her feet at the bottom, spun around and grinned at him. "Come on."

"When I get down there I want an answer, just so you know."

She crinkled her nose up at him but didn't reply, only motioned for him to get on with it. "Just get down here first, then we'll see."

Laughing at himself for being charmed into sliding down a child's slide he plunked himself down to the platform and gave himself a push. He laughed despite himself as he came to the end. "There, ya happy? If people from our high school could see me now."

"I think it just says you're fun-loving."

Standing, Trey walked up to her and pulled her into his arms. "Well, this fun-loving guy is hoping to get an answer. I don't want to be stepping on anyone's toes here. So do you have a thing for Ethan?"

She fingered the neck of his shirt, her eyes following her fingertips. "I did. I told him before I went away." She shrugged, and looked up at him. "But that was then." She forced a smile onto her lips. "And this is now."

"But you still have those feelings?"

"Is that relevant? He wasn't interested in me."

"Little bit. And I'm not sure that's entirely the truth."

Ivy's brow furrowed. "What do you mean?"

Trey thrust a hand into his dark hair, which was a tad too long, but looked bad boy sexy on him. "I mean… Fuck." He released her and took a step back, throwing his hands out to the sides. "Just forget what I said, I don't know what I'm talking about."

Her green eyes narrowed at him. "I think you do."

"Come on, let's take that walk on the beach." Trey turned, but Ivy grabbed his arm and forced him to stop walking and turn back to her. He didn't want to continue talking about Ethan, he regretted bringing up the topic in the first place, but just seeing her reaction gave him the information he needed. It was Ethan she wanted – not him. He was simply a distraction, a substitute, the runner-up.

"Trey." She placed herself directly in front of him. "I know we have a connection. We didn't before, but it's there now."

"But there's Ethan…" He could feel himself swaying. Of course it didn't help that she was looking up at him with those stunning green eyes and lips that had turned into a pout begging to be kissed.

"Listen, Trey. I want you." She stretched up against him, until her body was flush against his and ghosted her lips across his. "The question is, do you want me?"

The words had barely left her lips when he was pulling her roughly against him, devouring her with his lips. Fuck Ethan. He'd had his chance with her and blown it, Trey wasn't about to make the same mistake.

Ivy

"It's getting kinda chilly." Ivy snuggled closer to Trey as they lay on his leather jacket, watching the sunset, while reminiscing about old times and catching up on everything that had gone on in each of their lives in the past year and a half. The day seemed to fly by being with him. Despite the chill in the air it was easily the most perfect time of day; the streaks of red and orange and yellow in the sky were beautiful. While the sun's rays danced over the incoming waves, the individual drops of stray water looked like little diamonds dancing over the crests of the incoming tide.

Trey leaned over her and brushed a lock of hair from her face that a gust of wind had tossed over her eye. "Let's see what I can do about warming you up." He lowered his lips to hers. His lips hadn't even touched hers when a soft whimper escaped her lips in anticipation. He was such a passionate kisser, as if he put his heart and soul into each kiss, each caress. No wonder women fell over themselves for him. He pulled back and nipped at her lower lip as his hand caressed her side, just under her shirt, but not going any further up than her rib cage. It was like he had no urgency. It was driving her crazy.

Ivy grinned. "Better, but I'm still a little chilly."

She slid her hands under his shirt, feeling the definition of muscle in his back. "You're warm."

Trey lowered his mouth to her shoulder and placed a tender kiss there. "You know skin-on-skin contact is a much warmer option."

Ivy cocked a brow up at him. "Are you suggesting we get naked on a public beach?"

He looked up and made a show of craning his neck as if checking for other people. "Looks pretty deserted to me." He looked back down at her. "I'm just trying to give you options. That's all." He was in the process of lowering his lips to hers again when the sound of a phone buzzing came from his jacket pocket, just under Ivy's left hip.

Reaching into the pocket, Ivy grabbed the phone and passed it to him. His mother's name was lit up on the screen. He looked down at the phone and sighed, his mood becoming dour. "Dad's been…" he sighed. "I gotta take this."

Ivy didn't press. It was no secret growing up that Trey's father had a tendency to be abusive. When Trey was younger and still lived with his parents he'd come around with bruises; on a couple of occasions he'd even had a black eye. He'd refuse to talk about it but you would have to be stupid not to realize what was going on. Apparently, some things remained the same.

Chapter 5

Ivy

"Where's Trey?" Ethan asked, poking his head into Ivy's room an hour after Trey dropped her off. They'd stayed at the beach until sunset, cuddling and talking on the cool sand. It had been a wonderful day and she really didn't expect a man like Trey to be so romantic – he hadn't been before to her knowledge, but he was now.

Ivy looked up from the novel she'd been reading and caught Ethan's stare. He looked exhausted; he'd already stripped down to just a pair of jeans, the muscles in his chest and shoulders tight. Presumably another hard day. "He got a call from his mother. His dad's been drinking and getting rowdy. She asked him to drop in and defuse the situation. He assumed he'd be gone for the night. Said he'd swing by after his shift tomorrow."

"Ahhh." Opening the door wide, Ethan entered and crossed the room, sitting on the bed next to her.

"Ever think of knocking?" She motioned to the pair of Snoopy boxer shorts and camisole she was wearing, sans a bra. If you looked closely you could see the outlines of her large, dark areolas. "I'm not really dressed to be seen."

His eyes lazily took in every inch of her body, a cocky grin on his lips. "I'd beg to differ."

She averted her gaze, a blush forming on her cheeks as she shifted uneasily on the bed as the heat began to form between her legs. The way his eyes seemed to drink in every inch of her made her stomach do a little flip-flop. "What do you want?"

"What are you reading?" he asked as he made an attempt to grab the novel from her hands, but she jerked it out of his reach.

"None of your business." The last thing she wanted him to know was that she still read the corny romance novels he used to tease her about.

He frowned and made a swipe for the book. "Come on. Let me see."

She jerked it out of his reach a second time and put her hand behind her back. "No. You can't. Now scram." That was the last thing she wanted.

They stared at each other, neither one of them moving an inch. A slow smile crept onto his lips and she saw the devious gleam in his eyes.

"I said no."

He lunged, grabbing behind her back and yanking the book from her fingertips. With the prize in his hands he sat back and examined the cover. "*A Cop's Passion.* Sounds steamy." He wiggled his eyebrows at her and flipped to the page she'd bookmarked when he came in.

"Ethan! Give it back, you bully!" She lunged at him, attempting to get it back, but he held it out of reach.

"Nope, not until I see what's got you all hot and heavy."

"I'm not hot and heavy! Who uses that term aside from you anyhow?"

"Their eyes locked as she lowered her head and wrapped her lips around his large, throbbing cock..." he read, his smile so large it looked like his head was cut in half. "Well, little sister, I can't believe you're reading porn."

"It's not porn." She lunged again just as he was about to read another line and yanked it from his fingertips. "It's steamy romance."

"I don't know about that, but sounds like porn to me. That being said, you didn't give me much of a chance to evaluate."

With a groan, she swatted him on the shoulder with the book, her cheeks burning, turning a deep crimson. "That's why you're a bully."

"I'm not a bully!" A bark of laughter erupted from him.

"Bully, bully, bully." She whacked him several more times.

"Stop abusing me!" His laughter was contagious and she found herself laughing with him. "You're the one being the bully. I never assaulted you!"

She pulled her arm back to swat him again when he lunged at her hand. Ivy yelped as she went tumbling backwards, Ethan's body toppling over hers. The book fell from her fingertips as she squirmed under him until his body was situated between her legs.

Grabbing her wrists, with a little effort he forced them above her head and secured her wrists with his one larger, stronger hand. She continued to squirm under him, attempting to free herself, but all it managed to do was cause a hard ridge to form beneath the crotch of the jeans he was wearing.

Picking the book up with his free hand, he flipped to a random page. "*He entered her slowly, savouring the feel of her heat engulfing him, inch after blissful inch…* Kinda hot." He dropped the book by her head and looked down into her eyes. "So, does this turn you on?"

The look of desire that was flaring up in his blue eyes set her body aflame and she squirmed under him, not to escape, but so the ridge of his cock was settled against her mound. She moved under him again, the friction teasing her clit through the clothing.

"Does it?" All teasing was now gone from his eyes and all that remained was an intense hunger.

Ivy caught her lower lip between her teeth and moaned softly.

"God, Ivy…" He moved over her, grinding his hardened dick against her mound. Whether it was intentional or he was attempting to relieve the tension as she was, Ivy didn't know, but it sent a tremor of need through her. Her hands fisted above her head as she attempted to restrain her need to kiss him.

"Ethan, I –"

He lowered his head until his lips grazed her neck. "Ivy." He inhaled deeply. "You smell so good, I don't remember you smelling so sweet."

"It's been a long time," she managed to gasp.

He nipped at her neck, sending a jolt through her and she moaned, moving under him. It wasn't necessarily her intention to provoke him, in fact, she wasn't thinking much of anything as surges of need rippled through her.

"Ivy," he whispered as his lips and teeth made their way up her neck and along her jaw. He pulled up just enough to look deep into her eyes as he released her hands and ran his index finger along her collarbone. "I haven't been able to get you off my mind."

Her hands immediately went to his face. A slight beard had begun to form at his chin. She'd waited for so long to touch him like this and to feel his hard body covering hers. Slipping a hand to the back of his head she urged his lips down to hers. When his lips met hers it was like a dam had broken and the years of wanting and needing him surged through her in a ball of fiery need. The kiss wasn't sweet or intimate like it had been with Trey; it was fierce and urgent, like they were starving and the other person was their own source of nutrition.

Ethan's hand slipped between them, cupping her breast over the sheer material, as he ground his covered cock against her pelvis. Ivy wrapped her legs around his waist and pulled him tighter, rocking against the hard ridge of his cock. But she wasn't getting relief, instead it was only fuelling her need for more.

"Ethan. God, Ethan, what are we doing?" she moaned, pulling her lips from his and arching her back, giving him full access to her neck.

"What you've been wanting." His lips travelled down the side of her neck, nipping lightly at her ivory flesh. "What I've been wanting, I was just too stupid to realize it until now."

She lowered her hands to his shoulders, her fingers digging into the tight muscle as his lips reached her collarbone. As his lips trailed a string of kisses across her collarbone he pushed the hem of her camisole up and over her breasts.

The plan. This isn't part of the plan. His fingers pinched her nipple, then rolled it between his fingertips until it was a tight, dark nub, sending another surge of pleasure through her that made her pussy throb. *Fuck the plan.* Ivy moaned as Ethan's lips grazed her breast and tongue flicked the nipple.

The heat between her legs was becoming intolerable, demanding relief from the tension. Ivy's hands slipped down his well-defined, muscular back to the waistband of his jeans, slipping underneath the waistband and gripping his ass, pulling him down tighter to her.

Ethan released her nipple and his lips began travelling lower. Hooking his thumbs into the waistband of her boxers, he tugged them down. Ivy's body froze, her hands slipping to her sides, fisting the blanket under her, as she watched him slowly work his way down her stomach to the top of her shaven mound.

This. Her and Ethan. Was it finally going to happen… Now?

Trey!!! His name screamed out in her head. She groaned inwardly. This couldn't happen, at least not right now. She needed them both onboard to sharing and that wasn't going to happen if she let this proceed and caused a competition between them for her.

"Wait! Ethan, stop." Her body screamed out in protest as she grabbed his shoulders and pushed him off of her. "We can't."

He looked up at her, confusion and disappointment etched in his expression. But he didn't protest. Taking a deep breath in, he slowly released it and crawled up to lay beside her as she pulled her boxers back up and adjusted her camisole. She turned onto her side, propping her head up on her elbow. The throbbing between her legs was killing her, but she was pretty confident he was also suffering. At least they could suffer together.

"I'm sorry. I just think we shouldn't take this too quick. Not until we iron out a few things…" Not exactly true, but it would have to do.

"I get it." He began to sit up and leave when she grabbed his arm, pulling him back down.

"I don't suppose you'd be up to a horror movie marathon. Maybe some popcorn."

He laughed, mimicking her position on the bed. "Then we can have a good old heart to heart."

Ivy smiled. "Just like old times." She hoped. Really hoped.

Ethan looked over at the flatscreen television mounted on the wall at the foot of the bed. "Are there any good ones?"

"It's Saturday night, there have to be. And if not there's always porn."

"Oh yeah, that should keep my erection from bursting through my jeans," he groaned, rolling his eyes at her and flopping over onto his back. "Find a movie and I'll get the popcorn."

Ivy slipped to her back and laced her fingers behind her head as she watched him slide from the bed and undo his jeans, pulling them down. His erection, thick and rock hard, pressed against his boxer briefs.

"Wait, what are you doing?"

"You're in your underwear, why can't I be?" he protested. "Besides, I know I'll have no problem keeping my hands to myself. I think I proved that when you said stop and despite my extremely painful hard-on." He motioned to his crotch area, drawing her eyes to it. Hearing him laugh, she quickly averted her gaze, her cheeks growing warm. "Now, if *you* can't then that's not my problem."

She laughed. "Fair enough."

Ivy

It took every ounce of restraint within Ivy to keep from reaching across the bed and touching Ethan, or cuddling tight to him. Even sleeping Ethan looked sexy and powerful. Grabbing the remote she flicked off the television. Sometime throughout the night they'd fallen to sleep; she was pretty sure she was the first to go.

Looking over her shoulder she glanced at the clock on her nightstand. Shit, it was almost noon! Stretching on the bed, she attempted to work out some of the knots in her body. She hadn't exercised since she'd arrived home four days ago and it made her feel blah. Rolling over to wake Ethan, she reconsidered. He'd worked hard the previous night and didn't have to work today so there was no harm letting him sleep in, he wouldn't be sleeping this long if his body didn't need it.

Slipping from the bed she padded her way barefoot across the hall and into the bathroom. Stripping down she quickly brushed her teeth, used the facilities and then hopped into the shower. The warm, bordering on hot, water cascading down her back felt like heaven, like a gentle massage over her shoulders.

She'd just gotten shampoo in her hair when there was a ruckus in the hallway and the door to the bathroom burst open.

What in the hell!

She pulled the shower curtain back enough to poke her head out and immediately regretted it, quickly pulling it back in, blocking her view of Ethan. "What the hell Ethan!"

He groaned softly as he urinated in the toilet. "Sorry, but it was an emergency. I wasn't going to make it downstairs."

"That's gross, I'm trying to take a shower!"

"I'm not stopping ya."

She growled inwardly and stuck her head back out of the shower once the peeing sound ended to be replaced with the sound of the sink faucet being turned on. "Yeah, but I was having a relaxing moment in here. Then you came barging in without knocking. What if I was on the toilet?"

He grinned, turning off the faucet, wiping his hands on the pink hand towel on the countertop and catching her gaze. "I heard the shower, figured it was safe." He cocked a brow up at her, his grin widening. "And what do you mean by moment? Baby sister masturbating in the shower? I offered to take care of you last night, but you shot me down."

"I'm not really your sister, you realize that right? When you say baby sister you make it sound so incestuous and creepy. And kinda icky."

He shrugged, turning his back to the sink and folding his arms over his chest, but not making any indication that he planned on leaving anytime soon.

"What?" She wiped soapy water from her face. "Why are you looking at me like that?"

"I need a shower and you're in it."

"Take a shower downstairs."

"I prefer this one. The pressure is much better."

"I'm almost done."

Pushing himself away from the counter, he hooked his thumbs into the waistband of his boxer briefs and pushed them down. Ivy's eyes went wide as she watched his cock jerk alive, slowly thickening and growing to attention. "We can share."

Realizing she'd been staring, she pulled her gaze away from his dick and met his eyes, which were twinkling with humor. "But…"

He didn't give her time to protest as he crossed the room in two long strides, pulled the curtain open on the other end of the shower and stepped in.

"Whoa, wait, but…"

~*~*~*~

Ethan

Ethan's eyes scanned her, from her feet and slowly up until he reached her face. Her body was incredible, a shapely hourglass with just enough fat to give her a soft look; he was still having a hard time grasping the fact it was her. He had to admire the amount of hard work it must have taken to achieve what she did – he was damned proud of her. By the time his eyes landed on her face, her cheeks were a deep crimson colour.

As much as she pretended to be brazen and forward, the way she attempted to cover herself as he looked at her showed she still had the shyness in her he remembered from before she left. And he was happy for that. While he loved the changes in her, he'd cared for her before she left because she was a good, modest, fun person. It would have been a shame for that to have changed.

"Care to pass the shampoo?" He extended his hand to her and waited, his grin widening as she reached for the shampoo behind her and with a hand that trembled passed it to him. He intentionally dropped the bottle and it landed at her toes. "Shit. Clumsy." He closed the distance between them and bent until his face was level with her mound, the stream of water now hitting them both.

His cock jerked and throbbed. Maybe this was a bad idea. Correction, this was a very bad idea. He'd intended on making her suffer, but the suffering seemed to be one-sided. The temptation became too much. Leaning forward he pressed his lips to her mound and she uttered a little strangled, moan-like sound as her hands slid to his shoulders and her fingers dug in.

He wasn't sure if she wanted him to continue or not, but that wasn't the plan. The plan was to tease her, payback for the previous evening. He slowly kissed his way up her body, not stopping at her breasts despite the temptation, until his lips were covering hers.

Her hands slid around his neck, and she pressed herself tight to him as she gave herself into the kiss. Her lips and tongue tasted of fresh spearmint and the soft moans she made against his lips as their lips and tongues duelled tested every ounce of his restraint. There was nothing he wanted more than to hoist her up and onto his hips and slam into her, fucking her against the wall of the shower.

But then a thought came to mind – one he hadn't even considered. Was she still a virgin? He was pretty certain she was when she left for college, but that was well over a year ago, surely she'd had boyfriends at school. The thought of some random, faceless man fucking her pissed him off. He knew he shouldn't be envious, he'd fucked more than his fair share of women. Hell, when he and Trey were younger and stupid, it was a competition to see who could fuck the hottest girl. In retrospect, it seemed like such a stupid and shallow thing to do – the ambitions of a teenaged boy, he supposed.

He groaned inwardly. He had to stop this before he no longer had control over himself or the willpower to end it. If she was still a virgin he didn't want to take her virginity against the shower wall. Pulling away from her, he took a step back and squirted a dollop of shampoo into his hand and lathered up his hair.

"Ummm. Ethan?" she chewed at her lower lip, her gaze lowered to the shower floor.

"Oh, sorry. Want me to shampoo your hair?"

"I already did."

He shrugged, grabbed her shoulders and spun her around. His thinking was that not seeing the suds and water glistening over her breasts and mound would help lower his anxiety, but seeing her naked backside gave him thoughts of bending her over and ramming into her from behind.

"Yeah, but did you condition? It's all about the conditioner."

"Ummm." Her voice trembled, her breathing ragged as a slight laugh escaped her lips. He loved it. Every time she inhaled sharply it sent a surge of desire through him.

Placing the shampoo on the ledge to his right he leaned over her and grabbed the conditioner bottle. He quickly lathered up her silky strands, piling them onto the top of her head when done. He did his best to make the naked shower with her as platonic as possible. It was hard – fucking hard, but by the time they exited he was smiling on the inside. There was no doubt in his mind she'd be spending much of the day replaying the shower in her head – alas, so would he.

Chapter 6

Ivy

I'm the worst seductress ever, she groaned inwardly as she entered the living room with three beers in her hands. She passed one each to Ethan and Trey and kept the third for herself as she plunked herself down on the coffee table in front of them.

For a girl who had spent months planning and had her sights on getting revenge on the two playboys of Portland, Ivy was having some serious doubts on her plan. She didn't expect the men to have changed and she certainly didn't expect to have such intense feelings – both emotional and physical – toward them. They were amazing in different ways, Ethan was quiet and intense, while Trey was wild, yet tender.

She'd gone through the scenarios on how to approach the men about the threesome, but none of them seemed to be ideal. Maybe if she weren't falling for them both, but she was, which made making this work even more important. Her motives may have changed, but the end game was still the same.

So she'd made a decision; just say it and let the chips fall as they may. This needed to be brought up before an actual relationship developed between her and one of them. It had been so hard remaining a cool distance from them the past day after the intimate afternoon with Trey and night with Ethan. The only thing she knew for sure was that it needed to be brought up now otherwise rivalry might come between them. Her plan was never to come between their friendship, she couldn't be that vindictive.

"So ummm." The conversation between the two men stopped and they turned their attention to her, neither one of them saying anything.

Just say it Ivy!

"What's up?" Trey asked, a smile forming on his lips.

"Yeah, spill it," Ethan chimed in.

She took a deep breath in and released it in a loud huff. "Have you guys ever shared a girl?"

Their smiles faded and they stared blankly at her.

She paused, a part of her wanting to chicken out of the whole idea. "Ever? Like…"

Trey leaned forward on the sofa and braced his elbows on his knees. "When you say, share, you mean?"

"Like fucked one at the same time?" Ethan supplied, also leaning forward, eyeing her intently.

Oh this is hard. Oh my God, so much harder than I expected!

"You mean…" Trey's brow furrowed as he pressed his fingertips together and slapped the heels of his palms together. "Balls slapping together double fucking?"

"No." Ethan glanced over at Trey and shook his head. "No. We've never double fucked anyone. Is that really what you mean? Is that what you've been learning at college?"

"Wha–" Her mouth fell open. "No! I've never…" She ran a hand through her auburn hair. She could still feel Ethan's fingertips massaging her scalp that morning, it had been a horrible distraction the entire day. "I'm just asking."

"But why?" Trey asked, staring at her, his expression remaining blank. She hated that his expression was blank, she desperately wanted to know what he was thinking, good, bad or otherwise.

"Yeah, why bring it up?" Ethan added.

Just say it Ivy, what's the worst that could happen, a voice at the back of her mind said, *aside from them thinking you're some sex freak and ruining what you've gotten back from them.*

"I want to."

Their mouths fell open in unison and snapped shut in unison. They looked at each other, foreheads creasing. It was Ethan who broke the silence. "Ivy, we're not gay, babes."

"Just because you share a girl doesn't mean you're gay."

Trey pressed his fingertips together and made the slapping sound with the heels of his palms. "Balls. Slapping." He stopped the slapping motion and jerked his thumb toward Ethan. "And I don't want that dude's dick in my face."

"Your balls won't slap together, Trey," Ivy protested. "And why would his dick be in your face?"

"I don't know. Not sure I'm too keen on finding out." He grabbed his beer and downed it.

"I need more beer," Ethan announced, standing and exiting the living room without asking Ivy or Trey if they wanted anything.

Trey leaned forward and his gaze caught Ivy's. "Are you serious?"

Ivy didn't think her face could grow any hotter. She was so embarrassed she was actually beginning to perspire. *Well, no turning back now.* "Yes."

"But you've never…"

She shook her head. "I want to though."

Trey took her hands in his, forcing her gaze up to meet his again. "Why? I mean… Shit." He released her hands and raked a hand through his hair.

~*~*~*~*~

Ethan

She was going to give him a fucking heart attack. Maybe that was her plan after all, kill him via shock. Ethan opened a fresh bottle of beer and chugged half of it down immediately. Him, her and Trey? He'd envisioned her and him a thousand times, it felt like anyhow, since she came home, but Trey never entered the picture.

Admittedly, it wasn't the most *unappealing* idea. Sure, he wasn't keen on the whole "balls on balls" action that might be a possible side effect of the act, but it wasn't completely unappealing. It's not like Trey would be sucking his cock or anything. It would be all about her and he could only imagine the noises she'd make, the moans, the screams of pleasure. The thought was causing his cock to thicken. He finished the remainder of the beer, grabbed three more from the fridge and made his way back to the living room. Ethan gave Trey and Ivy new beers and sat back down on the sofa with his.

The thought that they'd been going through a ridiculous amount of beer crossed his mind for a fleeting moment. Although he anticipated many more in the near future considering the bombshell she'd dropped on him.

"If we could get past the mechanics of the act. Aren't we forgetting a very major thing?"

Trey and Ivy's eyes shifted to him, neither one speaking, both waiting for him to continue.

"Who gets Ivy? I mean, is this just a quick fuck deal or…"

"What do you mean, man?" Trey asked after a moment of silence.

"I mean, who's she really going to be with? Are we all going to be fuck buddies or is a relationship going to develop and one of us be an alternate to spice things up?" He looked directly at Ivy. "I'm past one-night stands and random fucks. I'm looking for the woman to spend the rest of my life with."

"We both are Ethan," Trey assured him, "but isn't that getting ahead of things a little bit? Neither one of us even knows what's running through her head right now."

"No, I don't think it is. I think it's sensible to consider what happens after. Just so there are no misunderstandings." Both men looked directly at Ivy, awaiting an answer.

Ivy looked from Ethan to Trey and back again. She raked her fingers through her hair and Ethan could see her hand shaking. He'd never seen her so nervous; not before taking her SATs, not before her prom, not even when she told him she was in love with him. "I want you both, in every way."

Trey blew out a loud huff of air and flopped back into the sofa. After taking a drink from the beer Ethan gave him, he cut his eyes over at Ethan. "What are you thinking?"

"I don't know. Maybe I'll be able to process this after the shock wears off." Ethan redirected his attention to Ivy. "Have you even had sex yet?"

Ivy huffed and scowled at him.

Ethan froze with his beer halfway to his lips, the his realization flaring up in his eyes. "You have had sex, right?" Sure, he'd suspected, but having her confirm his suspicions…

She got that uneasy look again, fidgeting with the family ring on her left middle finger – it contained the stones for her, her mother, him and his father. The ring had been a graduation present from him. It surprised him that she was still wearing it and hadn't pawned it or thrown it into the trash compactor after what happened between them.

Surprises are a dime a dozen today, I guess, he mused.

"Rock, paper, scissors on who gets her virginity," Trey joked, but his chuckling stopped immediately when Ethan shot him a dirty look and he pretended to have an intense interest in the list of ingredients on the beer label. "Just messing around," he grumbled under his breath.

"It's not like I'm completely stupid on sex. I've had oral. And I've used my vibrators more times than I can count. I've just not actually had a real penis –"

"Okay, stop." Ethan put his hand out. "We get it. Your pussy has seen some action. We get it. Although I'd like to know who these fuckers are that you sucked the cock of."

"Ethan!" Ivy glared at him. "It's none of your business. I don't ask you about all the women you've fucked. And I'm pretty sure your count is astronomical."

"Don't believe the hype," Trey cut in and chuckled.

"Not helping, Trey." Ethan gave his head a shake.

Ivy

"This was a bad idea, forget it guys." Ivy slipped from the coffee table and onto the sofa, between the men. "Let's just watch a movie or something." She grabbed the remote and began flipping through the channels, but slowed when she came to the adult channel, which featured a woman sandwiched between two men.

"First the books and now porn, Ivy," Ethan said and then cleared his throat.

"See, their balls aren't slapping together," Ivy pointed out, her index finger wagging at the television screen. "Not a single male body part is touching." She left the channel on for another minute, letting it sink in for the guys before switching to a new channel to a romantic comedy.

Not a single person spoke; they all pretended to watch the movie. However, if asked what it was about none of the three would be able to give an answer. At least not a correct answer.

Chapter 7

<u>Trey</u>

Trey couldn't keep his mind on anything other than the woman sitting between him and Ethan. Share her? He supposed that would fix the problem of having to slice her in half... That wasn't exactly what he'd had in mind. He hadn't really gotten that far really. His plan was to simply take things as they came. He looked over at Ethan, who was definitely further along than he was – more invested, although that was to be expected. That wasn't to say he didn't want something real with her, but considering this new information...

One thing was for sure, the tension in the room was so thick it was almost suffocating.

He looked down at Ivy. She was wearing a pink spaghetti-strap dress. The strap covering the shoulder closer to him had fallen off and was hanging on her arm. On impulse he leaned over and brushed his lips along her shoulder and to her neck.

Trey pulled away just slightly when she jumped at his unexpected contact, her head turned and her gaze caught his – her eyes questioning.

"Trey?"

Reaching out, Trey traced her jawline with his index finger and then caught her chin in his hand, tilting her face up to him. He lowered his lips to hers, as his hand slid along her face to the back of her head. He could feel Ethan's eyes on them, and to his surprise it was arousing to him. Maybe there was something to this.

She hesitated before responding, as if shy over the idea of kissing him in front of Ethan, which was almost humorous considering it was her idea in the first place. But it only took him sweeping the tip of his tongue along her lower lip for her to melt into him. She leaned into him, parting her lips and inviting him in as she turned to him, pressing the palms of her hands flat against his chest.

His need for her vibrated through him, his body needing more. Yearning to feel every inch of her naked body against his. Ivy moaned softly as his lips left hers and began to work their way along her jawline.

Ivy

Ivy could feel Ethan's eyes burrowing into the back of her head. She wasn't sure whether it was good or bad, but as Trey's lips began travelling along her jaw and to the side of her neck she turned to look in Ethan's direction and a surge of desire rushed through her as she saw the raw need in his blue eyes. It was stronger, more intense than she'd ever seen.

Working on instinct, she reached out and fisted the front of Ethan's shirt and pulled him toward her as Trey's lips reached the nook between her neck and shoulder, pausing there and biting at the sensitive flesh.

Ethan framed her face with his large hands, his eyes locking with hers. "This is crazy Ivy," he whispered, but didn't wait for a response as his lips came crashing down on hers with power and determination, as if he were attempting to rid her mind of Trey and claim her as his own. It didn't surprise her, she was sandwiched between two incredible alpha males, neither one accustomed to sharing.

He forced his tongue past her lips, to duel with hers. His mouth and tongue tasted of beer and peppermint – the flavour of gum he favoured. It was wild the stupid shit you remembered about someone you cared for.

Trey's hands slid to the back of her dress and inch by inch the zipper came down until the bodice of the dress was loose. Trey began working the spaghetti straps down her arms and then off, pushing the top of the dress to her waist, leaving her in just a strapless bra on her upper half. Her body froze upon realizing that this just might be happening; she should have been elated, but instead she was scared shitless.

Ethan's lips and demanding tongue, jousting with hers – along with Trey's hands, which were palming her breasts, turning her large, dark nipples into hardened peaks – brought her back to what was happening.

Ethan pulled back and looked down into her eyes. "Are you okay?"

"Yesssss." The word came out as a hiss.

"You still want to do this, baby?" Trey's voice asked from behind her before nipping at her earlobe.

Ivy looked over her shoulder at Trey. "I do. I'm…"

"I know." He grinned, releasing her breasts and cupping her chin in his hand and angling her mouth so he could plant a kiss on her lips. "But we'll be gentle." A devilish gleam mixed with the lust in his eyes. "At first."

"Come on, if we're going to do this I think upstairs would be a better place than the sofa." Ethan stood and extended his hand to her. She stood and her dress slid down her body and puddled at her feet on the floor.

"I don't think you'll need this either." Trey placed a kiss on her shoulder and undid the back clasp on her bra, freeing her breasts.

She immediately went to cover her breasts, but Ethan stopped her, forcing her hands to the sides. "I've already seen everything, honey."

Her face grew warm, flushing as she lowered her gaze.

"Wait, when?" Trey asked, slipping his arms around her and pulling her back tight to his front, kissing the back of her neck.

"This morning, in the shower," Ivy groaned, pressing back against him as the ridge of his long, hard shaft rubbed against her bottom through the layers of clothing.

Ethan laughed. "She shot me down though."

"Not for lack of trying," Ivy couldn't help but cut in, looking up to meet Ethan's stare.

"Can't blame a guy for trying."

"Well, in that case," Trey said as he bent down, put an arm under her back and one under her knees and hoisted her up into his arms. "I get to carry you upstairs."

Ivy squealed, squirming in his arms while linking her hands behind his neck. "Trey, oh my god, put me down, I'm too heavy!"

He cocked a brow up at her, a smirk forming on his lips. "Hardly. In fact, I think you might stand to eat a hamburger now and then."

She groaned loudly and rolled her eyes at him, as he followed behind Ethan up the stairs to the second-floor bedrooms. First I'm too fat, then I'm too thin, a girl can't keep up! But she couldn't help but feel good about the comment, or the fact he could effortlessly carry her up the stairs, held tight to his chest. Ethan led them into her bedroom with the queen-sized bed, removing his shirt as he walked past the threshold and tossing it to the floor.

Trey carried her over to the bed and tossed her onto it. She squealed as she bounced, her hair whipping into her face. She pushed her hair back to see Trey remove his shirt and leap onto the bed, covering her body with his own, settling between her legs. Heat radiated through him as her breasts became crushed under the weight of his muscular body. His lips worked down her neck and he moved lower, capturing one of her tight nubs into his mouth and circling the nipple with his tongue, sending delicious shivers of anticipation through her.

Ivy closed her eyes and moaned, giving herself a moment to savour the feel of his body and mouth on her. She opened her eyes and looked to her left, her stare catching her stepbrother's. "Ethan, come here." She reached out and grabbed Ethan's hand, pulling him toward the bed. When he got close enough she began fumbling with his belt buckle. It was so damned difficult, Trey's mouth slowly making its way down her body was so distracting.

Ethan chuckled at her attempt to free his cock. "I think you might need a little help." With his assistance she managed to undo his pants and yank them down just as Trey's mouth reached the top of her pink lace panties.

"God, I can't wait to taste you baby," Trey groaned, hooking his thumbs into the waistband of her panties and slowly pulling them down, kissing his way down her mound as it became available to him. The closer he got to the apex between her legs, the greater the ache of need became.

As Trey freed her of the final piece of clothing she had left on, Ethan crawled onto the bed and positioned himself at her shoulder, his already erect shaft bobbing just a few inches from her mouth. Grasping his cock in her hand, she began to stroke him from base to tip, her thumb circling the head, smearing the drop of pre-cum along the tip. Ethan moaned softly, his hips beginning to rock in her hand. She loved the power she had over Ethan; her strong-willed, sexy stepbrother was looking down at her with unrestrained passion and need.

Her attention was pulled from Ethan to Trey as Trey slid her legs over his shoulders and hoisted her bottom into the air. She watched, her eyes wide, her lips slightly parted as Trey spread her pussy lips and lowered his mouth to her mound.

"Trey, God Trey…" The wetness that had gathered between her legs was so uncomfortable. When Trey's tongue ran along the length of her slit she cried out, closing her eyes and arching her back. He licked her again, this time pausing to flick her clit with his tongue, sending a surge of desire through her.

As difficult as it was to keep any type of thought, she refocused her attention to Ethan, her grip on him tightening as she gently urged him closer, until his dick was in line with her mouth. Lifting her head she circled the head of his dick with her tongue, periodically flicking at the tip, lapping up the pre-cum as it gathered. Ethan cupped her breast in his hand, kneading the satiny flesh, his fingers pinching the nipple tight enough to send pulses of pleasure and pain through her.

"I want you to come in my mouth Ivy," Trey said, his voice laced with restrained hunger as his tongue probed her entrance a moment before he thrust it into her completely. His tongue thrust into her core just as she took Ethan's cock fully into her mouth, his cock muffling the sound of her scream of pleasure.

The pleasure coursing through her was unlike anything she'd ever experienced before. The hands of Trey and Ethan seemed to be all over her, touching, caressing, bringing her closer and closer to her breaking point. It felt so good she could barely focus on her mission to make Ethan come. She worked harder, her hand at the base of his shaft tightening around him and working in unison with her mouth, begging Ethan for his seed. As Ethan rocked against her mouth, she began to buck against Trey's thrusting tongue, the three of them working as one.

"Ivy honey, I'm coming. Let me go before –" Ethan attempted to pull from her mouth, but she kept him to her. His balls tightened and his cock throbbed seconds before an explosion erupted in her mouth.

She struggled to swallow him down, but managed. As she pulled her lips from him, Trey's torturous combination of tongue and fingers pinching her clit became her undoing; she closed her eyes and cried out as she released Ethan completely and fisted the blanket under her. Her mind was on one thing only, the pulses of pleasure rushing through her.

"Mmm, fuck baby, you taste good," Trey groaned as he lapped up her juices before slowly sliding her legs from his shoulders and laying her flat onto the bed. Once she was lowered to the mattress Trey moved back up the length of her body and claimed her lips with his as his rock solid cock slid between her legs, teasing her drenched slit, probing at her opening but not breaching the entrance. The taste of her juices greeted her tongue as she parted her lips, inviting him in, and she found it strangely erotic.

"Trey," she managed to gasp when he released her lips.

"Take her Trey, I'll join in when I'm ready."

Both Trey and Ivy looked over at Ethan, who was staring down at them, his dick barely half-mast. "I suggest you hurry, I won't be out of commission long."

Trey looked focused his attention on Ivy, placing his index finger under her chin and forcing her to look up at him. "You going to be okay?" Ivy was touched over Trey's concern and over Ethan's offer to stay at the sidelines – for now. If he'd said he wanted to be the first to enter her, there was no doubt Trey would step aside.

"Of course." She reached to the top drawer of her nightstand and pulled it open. Her hand rummaged through the drawer until she found a condom and passed it to him.

He grinned. "You've really thought this through, huh?"

She returned his smile and shrugged.

"Bad, bad girl." His shaft slid back and forth along her slit and the desire within her flared up again as he opened the foil package. Twenty years old and she was finally going to have sex with something other than her vibrator. With the condom on he pressed himself at her entrance. Her entire body tensed and she let out a strangled breath, her legs wrapping around his waist and arms tightening around his shoulders.

Trey took his time, slowly pressing into her, a soft groan escaping his lips. His glacial speed was driving her near insanity as she bucked under him, attempting to feel more – harder and deeper. But he refused to allow her control, making her wait, turning her into a ball of nerves.

"Trey, you're killing me," she groaned. Just as the words escaped her lips he slammed the rest of the way into her, making her scream out in surprise and pleasure, her nails digging into his shoulders. "Trey…"

Anything else she would have said was cut off as his lips came crushing down on hers. Ivy quickly lost herself in the feel of his body, his mouth, his tongue devouring her body. She began to move with Trey, their bodies working in unison, giving and receiving pleasure. The fire within her was burning to nearly unbearable heights, her body turning into a tight coil, ready to spring loose at any moment. Just when she was about to explode over his thrusting cock, she was jarred from her state of bliss as Trey rolled to his back, taking her with him, while keeping himself rooted firmly within her.

"Trey... Wha-" Opening her eyes she looked down at Trey, who was grinning.

"You can't come yet baby, you're missing someone."

Ethan! His name popped into her head just as she felt the bed behind her move and then Ethan's hands on her ass cheeks. A rush of fear raced through her. This was really going to happen. Both men. *Oh fuck, fuck, fuck.*

"Just stay calm. It'll be good once I'm in." Ethan's voice behind her was hardly reassuring.

Ethan spread her ass cheeks and the coolness of lube slid down her ass and into her slit. He gently massaged her ass, pressing at her tight, virgin hole with his thumb. Ivy groaned and collapsed onto Trey's chest as Ethan's thumb worked its way past the tight rim of muscle protecting her entrance and slowly into her.

"Breathe, baby," Trey whispered, nipping at the side of her neck, seeing and feeling the tension within her.

She was trying, trying so hard, but with Trey's cock in her and Ethan's thumb working her ass she was going out of her mind. Ethan's thumb joined by his index finger stretched her further, painfully far. She yelped, biting into Trey's shoulder to keep from crying out again.

Ethan removed his finger and she let out a sigh of relief, pressing her forehead to Trey's neck. But just as the relief passed through her, it was replaced by the need again – more intense than before as she moved back against Ethan, urging him to fill her again.

He didn't disappoint, but this time it was his shaft that pressed up against her back entrance – much bigger and stiffer than his probing fingers.

"Breathe," Trey said to her again.

As Ethan began to push into her, he slid a hand to her breast, pinching her tightened nipple. The feel of his fingers on her nipple sent a surge of need through her so intense that she bucked wildly against him, pushing his dick further into her ass. He gave a final push, groaning loudly, his fingertips digging deep into her hips. Ivy felt like she was going to be ripped in two by the two men's large cocks, but if she were to die at that moment she'd die happy as she remained on the crest of her arousal, so close to exploding her entire body hummed. Trey, Ethan and Ivy remained united, none of them moving for close to a minute, each indulging in each other.

"Are you ready?" Ethan asked from behind her, pushing her hair to the side and kissing her back shoulder.

"Yessss," she hissed though clenched teeth. As they moved, almost pulling out and then slamming back in again, she couldn't do a thing but hold tight to Trey and feel the waves of pleasure rushing through her and try to hold on just a little longer. But it was impossible, the two hard bodies that had her sandwiched, in combination with their moans of pleasure, so raw and primal, sent her tumbling over the edge. Her body convulsed and she cried out, but neither man slowed, in fact her release only made them fuck her harder, faster – relentlessly.

"I can't. Oh God," she groaned. The feelings rushing through her were nearly overwhelming her.

"Fuck, I can't even begin to describe how good your ass feels," Ethan whispered in her ear, reaching around her and palming her breast again, pinching her nipple, painfully hard, but she was already beginning the journey to another climax so she barely noticed.

"I'm so close, baby," Trey groaned. "Make me cum."

She clenched her pussy around him, milking him, begging him for his cum. But damn, it was so hard with Ethan slamming into her back entrance and Trey's cock throbbing within her. "I can–"

She was cut off as Trey fisted her hair and pulled her mouth down to his, kissing her almost violently. Their lips had just touched when she felt the pulsing within her and his low groan against her lips. His lips left hers and he pulled her down tight to him.

But it wasn't over, Ethan's thrusts came harder, faster, slamming her into Trey.

I can't take any more. God, I can't... The words were running as if on a loop through her head, but as the words came she found herself ready to come yet again. She dug at Trey's shoulders, leaving long gashes as Ethan slammed into her a final time and exploded. The feel of his cum heating her back entrance set her off a final time and she shuddered, too exhausted to even scream out, tears in her eyes and clinging to Trey.

As the last spurt of his seed left him, Ethan slowly and carefully removed himself from her and got off of the bed. Ivy collapsed on Trey panting hard, but with a wide smile on her face despite the teary eyes. She couldn't believe it had happened – was happening.

"How are you feeling?" Trey asked, rolling her onto her back and pulling out.

She smiled up at him. "Tired, sore, amazing."

"Hopefully not too sore," Ethan commented, lying down on the bed next to her and rolling to his side, facing her and trailing his index finger down her hip. "We're not near done yet."

Chapter 8

Ivy

Ivy awoke cuddled tight to Trey, her head resting on his shoulder and leg draped over his as his arm around her shoulders held her tight. She took a minute to admire him. He wasn't as broad as Ethan, although his muscle was more lean and defined. His cheekbones were also a little more defined and jaw angled whereas Ethan's was strong and square. She glanced over at Ethan, who was naked and spread eagled on the other side of her, sporting a semi-erection. The men were both so beautiful and sexy in entirely different ways.

She knew she was blessed. The luckiest woman in the world. The original plan when she'd arrived had been stupid and vindictive and the furthest thing from her mind now. It had been a very intense night and as she gently pulled away from Trey's embrace her body reminded her of the blissful abuse she'd received. Every muscle screamed in protest as she snaked herself off of the bed and stood at the foot.

Leaving the room as quietly as possible she made her way downstairs for a quick shower, hoping they wouldn't wake until she had breakfast prepared for them. She had the intention of serving them breakfast in bed, the least she figured she could do for the night they gave her.

After quickly showering, she wrapped a bath towel around herself and then made her way into the kitchen and skidded to a stop, a frown on her face as she planted her hand on her hips and eyed Trey in his boxer shorts already up and pulling ingredients from the fridge for breakfast. "Trey! What the hell?"

He deposited the mix of breakfast foods on the countertop by the stove and turned to face her, a wide grin spreading across his face. "Wasn't exactly the morning greeting I was hoping for, but all right." He gave her a wink and turned back to what he was doing, placing a frying pan on the stove top.

"No, I mean…" She sighed and walked into the kitchen and wrapped her arms around his waist, pressing her front to his back and placing a kiss on the back of his shoulder. "I wanted to surprise you with breakfast in bed. And you've ruined my plan."

He set down the knife he was using to chop up an onion and turned to face her, a grin still on his face. He looked so cute when he grinned, a hint of dimples appearing on his cheeks. "Well, if someone hadn't made such a disturbance getting off of the bed then maybe I'd still be sleeping." He bent and placed a quick kiss on the top of her nose.

Laughing she crinkled her nose up at him. "I was careful. But you had me in a death lock, it was hard getting away." She gave him a quick hug before stepping out of his embrace and surveying the ingredients he'd laid out on the counter. "Can I at least help?"

"That I wouldn't turn down." He finished chopping the onions and passed her a knife and some peppers. "Chop these up for the omelet."

They worked in silence. Once the breakfast was done with preparation and well on its way to cooking Ivy turned back to him. "Do you think this will work?"

Leaning his hip on the countertop, he crossed his arms over his chest and eyed her. "Oh, I think so, I always make this type of breakfast."

Grabbing a dish cloth she swatted him on the arm. "No, I mean. Us. Me, you and Ethan… Do you think it'll work?"

He clucked his tongue off of the roof of his mouth and his eyes left hers, seeming to focus on a spot on the wall above her shoulder and to the left. It was so long before he answered that she was starting to think he'd decided to ignore the question.

"I honestly don't know. This is real life baby, not some chick flick or romance novel."

Her brow furrowed. "What do you mean by that?"

Ethan lowered his gaze to meet hers. "I mean, I don't really know. As for me, the more I think about it, I like the idea. I care for you Ivy, always have. And I think I can be fine with sharing you with Ethan. I think." He chuckled. "Now that I know this can work without my balls touching Ethan's it's even more appealing.

Although I'm disgusted to say I got a taste of his –" he cleared his throat and pointed to his crotch "– little men when I kissed you. It was fucking gross. Now I know why lots of girls won't swallow."

Ivy groaned and rolled her eyes but said nothing.

"But Ethan…" He shrugged. "I'm not sure. He's in a different place than I am in regards to you."

"What do you mean?"

"Look, this isn't my place to say, but I'm starting to think Ethan doesn't have the balls to say it himself after what happened before you went to college and considering what happened last night. Well, fuck it. So here's the deal. Ethan's in love with you, Ivy."

Ivy's mouth dropped open. She wanted to say something, knew she should be saying something, but words didn't seem to want to come to her. Taking a deep breath in, she slowly released it and stared at Trey a moment longer.

"What do you mean?"

It was Trey's turn to look baffled. "Ethan's in love with you. What about that statement is tripping you up, love?" He turned to the skillet and focused on the omelets.

She gave her head a shake; the idea was silly. "Wait. How do you know that? Has he told you?"

"Not in so many words, but I know. He was miserable when you were gone. You shutting him out really tore him up. And part was guilt I'm sure, but now that I know what went down before you left, his reaction is clear to me. So when you ask whether this will work or not, it'll largely depend on whether Ethan is able to share the woman he loves."

"But he went along with it last night."

The cocky grin reappeared on Trey's face. "It's possible that he was horny and you said it was what you wanted and he just wanted to make you happy. I'm sure he enjoyed himself, sure seemed like it. But whether he could spend the rest of his life sharing you, I don't know. He brought up some valid questions. And he may ultimately force you to make a choice."

When she was making up the plan she never anticipated it going on for longer than a few group sex-a-thons and some dates. She'd only planned on letting it go on until they were smitten over her and then she was going to say goodbye. But now, she didn't want to say goodbye – not to either one of them – she truly did want them both. But could she insist on having them both if it hurt Ethan? She didn't think so.

"I'll talk to him." Looking up at him, she got up on her tiptoes and placed a kiss on his lips. "You're a smart, sweet, amazing man Trey Phillips."

Trey gave her another wink. "I'm not just a sexy body and pretty face, baby."

~*~*~*~*~

Wow. Ethan let out a loud huff of air as he sat up on the bed and looked around the deserted bedroom. *What in the hell just happened?* It seemed so surreal to him. He'd never dreamed he'd ever share a woman with Trey and certainly not Ivy and he wasn't exactly sure how he felt about it.

Standing he gathered his clothing and left the bedroom. Crossing the hall, he paused hearing Trey and Ivy downstairs. He couldn't make out what was being said, but the chatter was pretty lively – apparently neither of them had an issue with what had happened. He entered the bathroom and tossed his clothes into the hamper, then went directly to the shower, turning it on and hopping in.

He was just finishing when the bathroom door opened.

"Ethan?"

He laughed. "Who else would you expect to be showering in the bathroom?" Turning off the shower, he pulled the curtain back and flashed her a smile. She'd gotten dressed – sort of – wearing a pair of boxers and camisole, similar to what she'd been wearing the other night, but the camisole wasn't sheer and the boxers were a plain plaid pattern.

She shrugged, giving him a shy smile. He didn't miss the fact her eyes dipped to his groin for a split second. "I don't know. Guess it was a rhetorical question."

"How are you feeling?" Grabbing a towel from the overhead cabinet he wrapped it around his waist.

"Honestly?"

"Sure."

She crinkled her nose up at him. "Sore. Kinda confused."

A bark of laughter escaped him. "I could have guessed that." His laughter slowed as he noticed the smile fading from her lips. "What's going on?"

Placing her palms on the sink countertop she hoisted herself up and sat on it, letting her legs swing over the side. "Can we talk?"

He went to stand beside her and leaned into the mirror trying to determine whether it was worth the effort to shave. It wasn't. He pulled back and caught her stare. "Thought we were already talking."

She laughed and gave him a swat on the shoulder. "You know what I mean. Seriously. About last night."

"What about it?"

Her brow furrowed and she cocked her head to the side staring up at him. He could see her mustering the courage to say whatever it was that was on her mind.

"Come on. Spill it. What's going on in that pretty little head of yours?" He leaned in and placed a kiss on her temple.

"Were you okay with last night?"

He shrugged. "Sure. I suppose. It was a fun night." Despite his words, his dick jerked alive at being reminded of the previous evening. Hearing her moans and screams of pleasure was incredible.

"But how are you feeling about it?"

"Ahhh, so you want to talk about our feelings?"

She nodded.

"Kinda heavy for the day after isn't it?"

"Probably. But it's kinda important. Oh and just before I forget, mom and your dad called and they're extending their trip another week and a half. Apparently, they've fallen in love with Rome and want more time to explore it before carrying on to Venice."

"Uh, yeah. Nice topic detour."

She shrugged. "So what do you think? Would you be comfortable with the three of us –together?"

Ethan took a deep breath in and slowly released it, glancing over her shoulder at his reflection again. Could he really do it? He'd always thought he'd have a wife of his own and kids. The regular family unit, not him, his wife and his wife's husband. "It's... I don't know. My feelings toward it are complicated." But then again, he was getting ahead of himself. Severely ahead of himself. He was a planner, always had been a planner. How could he plan for something so insane? But an odd part of him found the idea interesting, perhaps something that could work. He certainly enjoyed the previous night much more than he expected.

"Because you're in love with me?"

His eyes shot to hers and he watched as she slapped her hands over her mouth and her emerald green eyes grew wide; apparently she was as shocked she'd said it as he was.

She kept her gaze focused on his and slowly lowered her hands. "I'm sorry, just Trey said..."

Ethan groaned. Trey. "Yeah, I swear to God Trey gossips more than a woman, no offense."

"None taken."

They continued to stare at each other. He could see the hopefulness in her eyes. Along with her feelings; they hadn't changed. He could see she was still in love with him, despite how he'd rejected her before she'd left. But she also had feelings for Trey now. She wasn't just his anymore and there was no turning back now.

"Is it true?"

He was the one to avert his gaze. "This whole thing has my head pretty fucked up."

"You're not answering the question."

"I know. Sharing someone I love wasn't something I ever considered doing, Ivy. Even if it is Trey." He ran his index finger along her jawline. "But I fucked up once and you're giving me another chance. So if that chance means sharing you, if that will make you happy, then it's what I'll do. I'll do it for you. Because, yes Ivy, I'm in love with you."

Chapter 9

Ivy

While his statement should have sent a rush of joy through her, it didn't. Trey had been right, he wasn't doing it because he was into the idea, he was doing it because it was what she wanted.

"I know what you're thinking." He spread her legs and stepped between them, grabbing her bottom and pulling her to him. When she looked up at him with questions in her eyes he continued. "You're thinking, I'm feeling backed into a corner and just giving in. That's not exactly the case."

"What do you mean?"

"I mean, even though I love you it doesn't mean I'd do something I wasn't comfortable with or agree with. Yes, I never thought I'd be sharing, but I'm willing to try and make it work. Had it been anyone else other than Trey, then no chance. But I'm willing to keep an open mind. I wouldn't have participated in last night had I been completely opposed to the idea. But you have my word, if I become uncomfortable with the idea, or feel it's too much for me then I'll bow out and Trey will have you to himself."

She didn't want him to bow out that way, she wanted him. But after the few days with Trey, she wanted them both. How could she be feeling this way about two men? It seemed so wrong. But it felt right. Would it be worth the risk of potentially losing Ethan forever to take a chance on the three of them?

"Breakfast is ready you two," Trey poked his head into the bathroom and announced.

Both Ethan and Ivy's heads turned to look at Trey – Ivy with a smile, Ethan with a scowl. "Doesn't anyone ever knock before busting into closed bathrooms anymore?" Ethan grumbled just loud enough for Ivy to hear, lowering his forehead to her shoulder. She had to bite down on her lower lip to keep from laughing.

Her eyes locked with Trey's. Sweet, fun-loving Trey. She knew she was being greedy, but she had to take the chance to have both men. Had to. Not because it was part of her stupid plan, but because she cared for him and needed him in her life.

"Oh, was I interrupting?" Trey gave them a lopsided grin, though didn't seem to be perturbed by his intrusion. "Didn't mean to. But didn't want to miss out on some potential shower action – we're a trio, right? And I think I'm behind a shower… And, like I say, breakfast is sitting on the table."

Ivy

"Is it all good? We one big happy trio?" Trey asked, motioning Ivy over to the hammock he was stretched out on. The day was beautiful, maybe one of the last beautiful, warm days until winter hit.

"I don't know." And she honestly didn't. She looked down at him in the hammock as he patted the area next to him.

"Come on, there's lots of room for us both."

Ivy laughed as she gingerly attempted to get onto the hammock with him. "I just don't want to send us both toppling to the porch."

"Ahhh, it'll be okay." He helped steady her as she crawled on next to him, nearly dumping them both onto the porch a couple of times, but after a minute of shifting and squirming Ivy managed to situate herself next to him, wrapped up into his arms.

"I don't know if it will. He said he'd try, but won't promise anything."

"Nothing in life is guaranteed, baby."

She looked up into his eyes and smiled. She supposed he was right.

"And what would you do if he decided to force you to choose? I told myself I wouldn't ask that and I've been thinking it's the noble thing to do and step aside, but I'm not sure I want to."

She looked up into his eyes and smiled. "I don't want you to." Her feelings and emotions were tearing her apart, she never expected this to be hard. She thought she'd hardened herself enough to be able to handle them both, but she'd been lying to herself. The only thing she wanted was to make them both happy. The fact they were both also in turmoil over this hurt.

"Good." He raked his fingers through her hair; the gentle pull of the strands of hair was oddly erotic and she closed her eyes, letting herself enjoy the feeling.

"Am I being selfish?"

"A little bit," he replied, not even slowing in his stroking of her hair.

Her eyes flew open and she picked her head up from his shoulder so she could stare at him. That wasn't the answer she was expecting from him.

Trey laughed. "I'm being honest. But I'm okay with it and I think Ethan will be too. Give him time. We've shared all kind of stuff over the years, why not a beautiful woman?"

"Goof." She gave him a swat, the quick and unexpected movement nearly toppling them onto the porch. "I'm serious."

"And so am I!" He slipped his hand behind her neck to bring her lips down to his when the sound of footsteps coming around the side of the house made them both freeze.

"Ivy? You back here?"

Ivy groaned inwardly as she let her forehead fall onto Trey's chest.

"That voice sounds familiar."

"It's Cassidy. I forgot I invited her over this afternoon." She looked back up and gave him an apologetic smile.

He sighed. "So much for my quality one-on-one action."

"Trey?"

"Please, like you weren't thinking it."

"Ahh there you are, why weren't you answering your phone?" Cassidy asked, coming into view.

"It's in the house," Ivy explained, untangling herself from Trey's embrace.

"Oh, am I interrupting something?"

"Yes, actually Cassidy, you are." Trey assisted Ivy from the hammock as he got out of it himself. "But I've gotta hit the gym anyhow."

Ivy shot Trey a scowl that he seemed to shrug off. Ivy didn't care for his comment towards her friend. Maybe he hadn't changed as much as he had let on.

"We'll talk later," Trey whispered in her ear as he bent and brushed his lips against her temple. "Okay?"

"All right."

"Cassidy." He gave Cassidy a final nod before leaving the women and making his way into the house.

"What's his problem?" Cassidy asked as the two friends made their way to a nearby picnic table and sat down across from each other.

Ivy's brow furrowed and she shrugged she was baffled and slightly pissed his attitude had been so cold that even Cassidy picked up on it. It certainly wasn't what she expected from the new and "improved" Trey Philips. "I'm not sure to be honest. Sorry about that."

It wasn't until the sound of Trey's motorcycle engine roared to life that Cassidy began with the questions that Ivy knew had been eating at her from the second she laid eyes on Ivy cuddled with Trey in the hammock.

Trey

Trey knew he'd been cold to Cassidy, it hadn't been her fault how things had played out, but it was easier than having to make awkward chitchat. He was roughly a mile from the house when the motorcycle seemed to choke up and the engine began to die, leaving him stranded.

Well, shit. He was too far from his own place to walk the bike there, so he turned it around and began walking back to Ivy and Ethan's. That was the better alternative anyhow, the trio planned on spending the night together so maybe once Ethan got off work they could spend an hour trying to figure out what in the hell was going on with the bike.

At least I'm still getting my workout, he grumbled under his breath as he pushed the bike up the final hill and the house came into view. The final few yards up the steep hill were torture; by the time he wheeled the bike into the driveway and put the kickstand down he was panting and sweating profusely.

He made his way around the side of the house and as he came up to the backyard, his steps slowed hearing his name being said. He stopped completely when he heard Ethan's name mentioned. He knew he shouldn't eavesdrop, but he was curious as to how Ivy was explaining the situation to her friend, if she was explaining it at all.

Cassidy: So how are they?

Silence.

Cassidy: Come on, tell me. I'm dying to know. Like, how do you make it work?

Ivy: It was good. Kinda odd at first, but good.

Ivy giggled.

Ivy: Okay, it was mind-blowing. I'm so glad I waited.

Cassidy (with wonderment in her voice): So, they both agreed to share you.

Ivy: Yup, I mean… It's been a little up and down. Trey's more into the idea than Ethan, but I think they're both on board.

Cassidy: I gotta admit, I had my doubts you could do it, but you have my admiration, girl.

There was a soft clapping sound that Trey assumed to be the girls high-fiving.

Trey frowned. What in the hell? Did Ivy come home having this planned all along? Sure, she'd been rather forward, but with the weight loss and coming home with a new sense of confidence he didn't doubt she'd have the courage to go for them both. But still? It didn't sit right with him.

Ivy: It was nothing. And it's not like that.

Cassidy: So are they really falling for you, or is it just sex?

Trey's jaw clenched at the tone in Cassidy's voice. Sure, Cassidy had a reason to be bitter, at least with Ethan, but what in the fuck did he do to her – sweet fuck all, that's what.

More silence.

Cassidy: I know that look on your face, spill it.

Ivy: Ethan said he was in love with me this morning. Said he's been in love with me for a long time. Trey and I are just starting to connect. It's complicated.

Cassidy: Ahhh, well, it's Ethan you really wanted to hurt, Trey was just a happy addition. I wish I could be there when you dump their sorry asses and they finally get what's coming to them. Your plan was brilliant. Truly inspired.

Trey froze; it felt like the blood in his veins had turned cold within him. A part of him wanted to storm into the backyard and demand answers from Ivy. But another part needed time to ponder what was being said, perhaps discuss it with Ethan first. Disgusted with what he'd heard and having no desire to hear more – he'd heard enough – he spun on his heel and made his way to the front of the house and entered through the front door. He'd pretend he hadn't heard the women's conversation and have a chat with Ethan when he got home.

Then they'd deal with Miss Ivy Sullivan as a team. She wanted two boyfriends, well, now she had to deal with them as a team. She'd always been such a sweet, honest woman… How in the hell did she come to be so vindictive? It was sad and disappointing.

Chapter 10

<u>Ivy</u>

"Did you hear that?" Ivy spun around on the bench and looked to the walkway that led around the side of the house to the front yard.

"Hear what?"

Getting up from the bench and walking across the backyard to the walkway, she peeked around the corner. It was deserted. She shrugged. "Nothing I guess, I thought I'd heard footsteps."

"I think it's your imagination." Cassidy motioned for her to come back to the picnic table. "So come on, so tell me, how are you going to do it?"

The conversation was making her uneasy. "I don't think it's such a good idea, Cassidy." She shrugged. "I mean, it seemed like a good idea at the time, but –"

"What? I don't –" Her expression turned to one of confusion, mixed with disappointment.

Surprise Ivy got, disappointment – not so much. Why would she be disappointed? She didn't have a horse in the race. What would it matter to her?

"What aren't you telling me, Cassidy?"

Her friend frowned and lowered her gaze, staring at her hands.

"Come on. Be straight with me. Whatever it is I won't be mad, or… I don't know."

Her friend took a deep breath in and slowly released it. "Okay. I'm really sorry, Ivy."

Ivy wanted to reach across the table and shake her friend for being so cryptic, but instead she covered her friend's hands with her own. "What did you do Cassidy?"

"Please, promise you won't be mad. I made a mistake."

Ivy had no idea what this secret was but she was getting pissed. Really pissed. Cassidy wouldn't be beating around the bush if it wasn't something that would really upset her. "What. Did. You. Do. Cassidy?"

"I slept with Ethan."

Ivy jolted upright as if she'd been invisibly slapped, pulling her hands from Cassidy's. And in a way she had been. A thousand questions raced through her head as she stared at her friend. How could she? How could he? And how could they not tell her! She swallowed down her anger and hurt, taking a deep breath in and slowly releasing it.

"So it was like a one-night thing? Like, when did this happen?"

Cassidy's gaze slid back to her hands. "I'm sorry."

"I don't want to hear 'I'm sorry,' I want to hear when this happened," she snapped, then silently chastised herself for letting her temper get the best of her.

"After you left."

Well, I could have guessed that, Ivy silently fumed, getting more and more pissed at her friend's reluctance to just give her the desired information. How fucking hard could it be to just fucking say what she wanted to know?

"I mean, exactly. When. Exactly."

Cassidy shrugged. "Maybe a week."

Ivy received another sharp jolt of hurt. A week. A week! She'd poured out her heart and a week later Ethan was fucking her best friend.

"We met at a club and he was upset."

"So you were his shoulder to cry on after rejecting me?"

"He was pretty upset you were ignoring him."

"He broke my damned heart Cassidy! No wonder." As she said the words she wondered if that was why Trey was so cold with Cassidy. He knew she'd been fucking Ethan and it made him uncomfortable. So three... Three people who claimed to care for her were keeping a big, fat, painful secret from her.

Cassidy cringed. "I'm just saying, he was upset and we started talking and getting to know each other."

"How does it go from being friends and consoling each other to fucking?"

She shrugged. "We were attracted to each other so we started seeing each other."

"Dating?"

Cassidy gave her a sympathetic smile. "Sort of. We didn't tell anyone 'cause we didn't want to hurt you. But I felt you should know. We're best friends and I couldn't keep this secret any longer and didn't want you to hate me if he was the one to tell you first."

Ivy huffed. "So why did you two break up?"

Cassidy sniffed and wiped at her eyes with the back of her hand. "He dumped me. He threw me away like a piece of trash when he got bored of me. Just like all the other women he's ever dated." A flash of venom shone in her friend's eyes. "That's why I'm glad you're doing this. So they'll know how it feels to be insignificant and tossed away after giving their heart to someone. Ethan never cared for me."

A part of Ivy was glad Ethan never cared for her friend – a sliver of juvenile satisfaction. She'd been hurting from Ethan's rejection and the people she loved had found each other, comforted each other. It felt like such a betrayal.

"We're okay, aren't we Ivy? I wanted to tell you, but I was scared you'd hate me. I know how in love with him you were."

Am. I still am. Ivy sighed. She had no idea how to process this new information or what to do with it. Did it change the present? How could it not?

"Does Trey know?"

"Yeah, I think so."

"How long did you two date?"

"A month. Maybe."

Ivy chewed at her lower lip. A month. She would have fucked him at least a dozen times. She looked up into the window that belonged to Ethan's former bedroom. Did they fuck in the room she told him she loved him in? He would have been in the process of moving at the time they dated. Did they fuck in the shower? Did he touch Cassidy in the same manner? Shampoo her hair? Caress her body? Just like he had with her… She wanted to know, but she didn't. The details would kill her.

"What are you thinking, Ivy? Please talk to me." Cassidy reached across the table and took her friend's hands. "You're over him, right? So it doesn't matter… Right?"

Ivy forced a smile onto her lips. It was such a forced smile her face actually hurt from the action. "Of course. It's fine. We're good."

~*~*~*~*~

<u>Ethan</u>

"Is Cassidy here?" Ethan asked as he walked into the house and was greeted with Trey, who cornered him in the foyer.

"Yeah, she is."

Fuck, Ethan groaned inwardly. He figured he'd run into Cassidy eventually, it's not like Portland was a very big city, but was hoping it was later rather than sooner.

He gripped the back of his neck and attempted to loosen the knot that was beginning to form. "Where are they? What are they talking about?" Ivy hadn't mentioned his dating Cassidy so he assumed Cassidy had kept their deal and not said anything. He'd planned on telling Ivy, but the time just wasn't right. She'd just stopped hating him and things were beginning to work for them. He wanted to make sure he was on solid ground with her before rocking the boat.

Trey's mouth formed into a tight line and his brow furrowed. He was angry. "It's all a game, Ethan."

"What?"

"A game. I don't know the details, they didn't know I was listening and I left before I got caught eavesdropping, but I heard enough Ethan."

Ethan pulled off his jacket and hung it in the coat closet, confused. "I have no idea what you're talking about, man."

"I mean, Ivy is fucking with us."

Ethan's frown deepened. "Fucking with us?"

"As in she set this whole thing up. She came home just to make fools out of us by making us share her. Apparently she plans on dumping both of us. Cassidy knew about it so I would guess this is some little plot they hatched up together."

The whole thing sounded so ridiculous that Ethan laughed. "Ivy wouldn't do that."

"I know what I heard, man."

"Then you heard wrong." Ivy wouldn't do that. Period. He had no desire to even indulge in the notion. Ethan made an attempt to move past Trey, but Trey blocked his path.

"I know what I heard. Cassidy seemed excited over the idea and Ivy didn't deny it."

"I know Ivy. She's a kind, smart, beautiful woman. She would never do that."

"You knew Ivy. KNEW. We're different people now and it's not exactly all that farfetched to think that perhaps she's changed as well. For all we know she has some boyfriend on campus and we're just the entertainment for a few weeks. Come home, humiliate us, then go back to her life with some college frat douche."

Ethan slowly shook his head. He couldn't even conceive of the notion. Yes, it was strange that she suddenly wanted them both. Yes, she did seem to move quickly. Yes, she did seem to forgive him without giving him too much grief… All of those things when put together did seem a little odd. But to think Ivy was plotting against them? Bullshit if he'd ever heard it.

"Is this some sort of play for her?"

Annoyance flashed in Trey's eyes. "What? Play for her?"

"Yeah, you want me to go off the handle, accusing her of some crazy conspiracy theory to humiliate us so she'll go running to you, because… surprise, surprise, Ethan's an asshole – yet again."

"Look, I'm not saying we ambush her. I'm saying we discuss it with her. And just to remind you, I was the one to embrace this idea first. Not you. You're the one that's fucked in the head about it."

Ethan's fists clenched at his sides as he fought to calm his temper. "I'm not…" He gave Trey a not-so-gentle shove out of the way and proceeded around him. "I need some time to think about this."

"I'm just saying we need to sit down and discuss this with her, man. Get the truth out and then decide how to proceed with this – together."

"Just give me a bit to mull it over." He pushed past Trey and made his way into the living room, flopping down onto the sofa, pulling off his boots, kicking them under the coffee table and then flipping on the television. He wasn't in the mood for Trey's bullshit. If this was the kind of drama that was going to come from the three of them involved in a relationship then it wasn't going to work. She'd have to make a choice, which was unfortunate since he was honestly beginning to warm up to the idea – despite the potential complications.

Chapter 11

<u>Ethan</u>

But what if it was true…

"I'd buy that you're just making this shit up to get Ivy and I fighting before I'd believe she'd do something like that," Ethan stated, not looking over his shoulder when he heard footsteps entering the living room behind him, assuming it was Trey. He had no idea how much time had passed from the moment he sat down and now, if someone had tested him on what he'd watched on the television he would have failed the test miserably. If he were forced to guess, he's say maybe a couple of hours.

"Do something like what?"

Ethan's head spun around to see Ivy entering the living room. Where Trey or Cassidy had gone was beyond him. "Where's Trey and Cassidy?" Not that he really fucking cared one way or another.

"Cassidy went home. I didn't know Trey was back from the gym yet."

Ethan turned back to stare at the television screen. Some sitcom was on. He didn't know the name, had never seen it before that moment. "Yeah, he's here. Was here. I think. I don't know."

She walked into the living room and plunked herself onto the coffee table, directly in front of him, blocking his view of the screen. When his eyes met hers he groaned inwardly; it looked like she'd been crying. He knew why.

Him. Again.

He'd fucked up. Again.

Cassidy had been there, they'd been chatting. No doubt Cassidy spilt the beans on their brief relationship – although it was so brief he hesitated to even classify it as one. Even if Trey had been right, maybe he deserved whatever plan she had in the works.

"What's wrong?"

She laughed, but it was a hollow, joyless sound. "Why did you do it?"

He took in a deep breath and slowly released it. "Do what?" He felt stupid even asking the question, they both knew what, the words kinda just fell from his lips.

"With my best friend. A week after I left. Was it not enough to break my heart, but you felt the need to rub my nose in how inferior I was? How unworthy? How could you?" She sniffed and wiped at her eyes with the back of her hand. The waterworks were about to start again.

"I was stupid, Ivy. I was messed up. You were ignoring me."

Her eyes widened, filling with anger. "So you felt the best way to gain my attention was to give Cassidy what I wanted?"

"We fucked, Ivy. A few times. It wasn't a relationship, it was a release. A way to get you out of my head. Nothing more or less."

"It didn't feel that way for her. You hurt her."

Ethan leaned forward, throwing his hands out to the sides in surrender. "Guess that's what I do. I was an asshole. Am an asshole. I break women's hearts for sport." His jaw clenched as a fresh batch of tears streamed down her cheeks. He sucked at relationships. He wasn't smooth like Trey, he didn't always know the right things to say to make things better. "I didn't promise her anything, Ivy. She knew I wasn't ready for anything serious."

"And so you decided it would also be a good idea to keep it from me. All of you did. You, Cassidy, Trey. You all lied to me."

"When was a good time to bring it up, Ivy? When you hated me? When we were finally getting past what I did? When I was fucking you, with my best friend might I add? When would have been a good time to say 'Oh Ivy, by the way, I had a fuck fling with your BFF, thought you should know.'"

She stood suddenly and turned to rush from the room, but Ethan wasn't letting her go. Not again. Last time she ran she was gone for well over a year. Leaping from the sofa he grabbed her upper arm, stopping her and spinning her back around to face him.

"I'm not letting you go. Not again. We're going to discuss this and make it right." He stared into her eyes and he saw a shimmer of guilt. Just a smidge, but enough to consider that what Trey said may have been true. He wasn't the only one being dishonest in this relationship.

A voice in the back of his mind screamed at him to confront her about Trey's allegations. But he wasn't sure if he could – or should. If the answer was "yes" he didn't know if he could handle the truth, he'd opened his heart to her and been willing to do anything to make her happy. But just because her original intentions may have been less than honest that didn't mean they couldn't have changed. And if they'd changed then that should amount for something, right?

"Let me go, Ethan!" She attempted to pull her arm out of his ironclad grip, but he refused to release her even though he feared he may be leaving a bruise.

"No, there's no way in hell I'm letting you go again. Not like this."

"Please." Tears were flowing freely now and she didn't even try to wipe them away as she glared up at him. "I can't get the image of you fucking Cassidy out of my mind! It sickens me."

A smirk turned up the corner of his lips and he shrugged. He didn't know why he smiled, it was just a stupid reaction to a heated situation. "Funny, you had no problem letting me watch as Trey fucked you and ate your pussy. Double standard or all a part of the master plan?"

The slap came so suddenly and so unexpectedly he immediately released his grip on her arm and touched the side of his face where the palm of her hand had once been. He was in complete and utter shock. Sure, it wasn't the first time he'd been on the receiving end of a scorned woman's palm, but he didn't expect it from Ivy. And the woman had put some power behind that slap, it stung like a son of a bitch. Their eyes locked and he knew what Trey had heard was the truth.

"Fuck you, Ethan!"

She stormed off, rushing up the flight of stairs and moments later her bedroom door slammed shut and Ethan was hit with an uncanny sense of da-ja vu.

Trey

"What's wrong with it?"

Trey looked up from his partially disassembled motorcycle to see Ethan at the garage doorway that led to the foyer. He motioned to the bike with a look of disgust. "Fuck if I know."

Ethan laughed as he walked into the garage and crouched down beside Trey. "Then why is it in pieces on the garage floor?"

"Needed something to do. You know, keep my mind busy while I sort out some shit."

"Want some help?"

Trey laughed. "You certainly couldn't make it any worse."

Despite his offer to help, Ethan didn't even attempt to touch the bike. Instead, he stood and leaned back against Ivy's car, crossing his arms over his chest and giving his head a shake. "You were right, you know."

"Oh." Trey sighed. Normally he'd be happy to hear Ethan admit he was right about something, but this wasn't one of those instances. "I didn't want to be right. I was hoping there was an explanation. Or maybe I'd heard wrong or… something." He stood and wiped his hands on his jeans. "What did she say?"

"After she slapped me she took off upstairs and locked herself in her bedroom. I didn't get an explanation."

Trey frowned. "And you let it go at that?"

"She's fucking locked herself in her room and refusing to come out. She won't even yell at me to go fuck myself when I pound on the door for her."

"And you're just going to let it go like that?" It wasn't near good enough for Trey. Not even close.

"I can't force her to talk to me."

"Yeah, ya can. It's what you should have done last year."

Trey turned, intent on going to see Ivy, if it meant taking the door off of the hinges then so be it, but Ethan's hand on his arm stopped him. "Before we go storming up there intent on breaking shit down, don't we have something we need to work out first?"

"What?"

"Whether we are really willing to do this."

He was, there was no longer a doubt in his mind. The fact Ethan was there discussing Ivy with him, as if she were their problem – not his, THEIRS – told him everything he needed to know. "Yeah. I am. And quite frankly I don't think you can handle the new and improved Ivy on your own." A grin formed on his lips. "I really think this needs to be a tag-team effort."

"Are you sure? We can't be flippant about this. If there's more to this than just her little scheme to get even with us and she does in fact have feelings for us both, we need to be sure we're fine with that."

"For the last time. We're cool. We've shared everything else since we were kids anyhow…" He jerked his head toward the direction of the house. "Now can we go get our woman back or do you want to continue with this circle jerk?" Trey started toward the door and stopped suddenly, nearly being knocked over and onto his ass as Ethan collided into him.

"Shit. Sorry."

"Fuck man. A little space please." Trey took a couple of steps backwards and motioned to the space between them. He proceeded to move past Ethan and to Ivy's car. Popping open the hood, he removed the sparkplugs and stored them in the pocket of his motorcycle jacket, which was hanging over the handlebars of his bike.

"What are you doing?"

Trey grinned. "She's a runner isn't she? She's not getting back to Boston anytime soon without spark plugs."

Ethan looked like he was about to protest and then stopped, confirming Trey's decision with a curt nod. "Good call. But when she flips out, I had nothing to do with it. You're riding that out on your own."

Suddenly, something popped into Trey's head that he felt needed to be said, and now seemed to be as good as a time as any. "And FYI, ya need to lay off of the red meat and maybe start eating more kiwi."

The look of confusion that came upon Ethan's face was priceless. "Why in the fuck would I do that?"

"Because your jizz tastes horrible and I honestly have no idea how Ivy can swallow that shit without gagging."

All colour drained from Ethan's previously bemused face. "How in the fuck do you know that, asshole?"

Trey chuckled, but didn't bother responding. Having to taste Ethan's "storm troopers" on Ivy's lips was almost, *almost*, worth seeing the expression in his friend's face as he processed that comment. Almost.

"Hey, seriously. Did Ivy say something to you?" Ethan called after him. "You just can't say fucked-up shit like that to someone and walk away!"

Ivy

"Go away, Trey!" Ivy shouted through the door.

"Look, Ethan isn't with me."

She wasn't sure if she was more upset or relieved that Ethan hadn't persisted with his pounding on her door. But then again, why would he? He hadn't last time, aside from a few half-hearted knocks on her door, and he hadn't this time. A few half-assed knocks and that was it. His actions spoke louder than any words he could have said. She wasn't worth fighting for.

But Trey was there. Trey… Sweet, fun, wildly unpredictable Trey was there. Didn't she at least owe him an explanation?

"Fine." Sliding from the bed, she slowly made her way toward the bedroom door and paused with her hand on the handle. "Are you sure Ethan isn't with you?"

"Would I lie?"

Yes, he would and he did. But she supposed he hadn't lied technically, he just didn't tell her Ethan and Cassidy's secret. Unlocking the door she pulled it open and came face to face with Trey.

"Thanks. I think we all need to just sit down and discuss this." He walked past her and into her room, followed my Ethan.

Planting her hands on her hips she glared at Ethan. "I thought you said the Judas wasn't with you, Trey!"

Ethan spun around and met her glare with one of his own. "Did you seriously just call me a Judas? I think that's a little harsh."

She cocked a brow at him but didn't respond. Admittedly, she overstepped a little with that comment, but her pride refused to allow her to take it back.

Trey grabbed Ivy's hand and pulled her further into the bedroom and steered her over to the bed, forcing her to sit down next to him. "All right. We're all adults here. And we need to just sit down and get this sorted out." He looked from Ivy to Ethan, who was reclined against a wall, his arms crossed over his chest, and back again to Ivy.

"He lied to me," Ivy spat, her glare remaining on Ethan.

"You lied to us both," Ethan retorted.

"I did not."

"So you didn't have this planned with Cassidy?"

"No, I didn't."

"Really? 'Cause this plan has Cassidy written all over it."

"Really," she confirmed with a nod of her head. "Thought of it all by my little old self. Not too bad for a girl flunking out of college, huh?"

Ethan's mouth dropped open. "You're flunking college, Ivy? Flunking! You said you weren't doing so good. Flunking isn't doing not so good. Flunking is doing awful. What in the hell, Ivy!"

"Oh, don't get so melodramatic, Ethan. Like you really care."

"Fuck Ivy, of course I care. How many times do I have to tell you I love you for you to get it through your thick skull?"

Chapter 12

Trey

Trey placed his face into the palms of his clasped hands and groaned inwardly. The two of them were going to cost him his sanity, he was sure of it. They had to be one of the most dysfunctional trios of all time. After allowing them to bicker like an old married couple for over ten minutes he stood, placing himself between them, attempting to defuse the situation.

"Let's try this again."

Ivy cocked a crow at him and shrugged. "Fine."

He directed his attention to Ethan, who nodded his compliance.

"All right." He focused his attention back to Ivy. "Look, love, we've done some stupid shit. I'll admit it." He jerked his thumb toward Ethan. "And I think somewhere between the two of you throwing insults and accusations at each other he admitted it."

"Funny, that's not what I heard. I heard a lot of nagging. A lot of scolding. That's what I heard."

Ethan threw his hands up in the air and glared at Trey. "See. I told you. There's no reasoning with her when she's like this."

She huffed, jumped to her feet and stormed out of the room. "I'm done."

~*~*~*~

Ivy

Ivy banged on the steering wheel with the palms of her hands. Why in the hell wouldn't it work? Of all the luck, she was stranded there.

She sat in the car for close to twenty minutes attempting to sort out the mess her head was in. As her temper began to calm she began to see things a little more clearly. They'd all fucked up. And yeah, she may have deserved the lecture. It was Ethan's way. He cared about her future and sometimes he came off a little abrasive – more abrasive than he intended no doubt.

But I'm not totally innocent here either, she mused.

The three of them had been so fixated on arguing about what Ethan had done and her lack of dedication to her scholarship that they hadn't even really touched on her little deception – okay, big deception.

She looked at the garage door and then back at her steering wheel. Running away wasn't the answer, it was a cowardly thing to do.

But what if they hurt me? The question came to the forefront of her mind. Being hurt by Ethan was one thing, but both of them? It would be devastating. It was easier to run.

But she didn't want to leave them. And it appeared she wasn't going anywhere anyhow. She opened the car door and as she was sliding out from under the steering wheel she noticed Trey's bike in some stage of being fixed. He'd been tinkering in the garage all afternoon.

Closing the car door she clucked her tongue off of the roof of her mouth. The car had been working fine until this afternoon.

Dirty buggers!

Now she knew why they hadn't run after her. They knew she couldn't get anywhere. Instead of being angry she smiled, giving her head a shake in disbelief. Heading back into the house she didn't have to go far to find them. They were both sitting in the living room watching some action movie.

She stood in the entryway of the living room, her hands planted on her hips, looking from one guy to the other and back again. "Who messed with my car?"

Trey was the first to turn and greet her with a smile. "Something wrong with your car?" He was a lousy liar. Absolutely horrible.

"Yeah. Doesn't work."

"Maybe you ran out of gas?" Ethan offered, turning as well and also giving her a smile.

"I don't think so."

"Humm. That's weird." Trey's grin widened as he looked over at Ethan and they shared a look. "Guess you'll have to come on in and keep talking to us until this is worked out."

She cocked a brow up at him and fought to keep a smile from her lips. "I can get to Boston other ways you know."

"Yeah, you can totally hitch. I wouldn't recommend it." Trey pasted a look of disgust on his face and shook his head.

"Or a bus," Ethan chimed in.

"Oh hey," Trey reached across the sofa and swatted Ethan on the shoulder. "I saw a bicycle in the garage. That could work too." They began chattering among themselves, discussing the possibilities as if she weren't there glowering at them both.

Entering the living room, she plunked herself down onto the coffee table in front of them. "Okay, I get it! I don't really have to be here if I didn't want to be."

Ethan's expression turned serious as his eyes locked to hers. "Then what are you saying, Ivy? Everything considered. No more games. So what do you *honestly* want from us?"

"We want the truth. Is it real or some game you're playing with us?" Trey added for clarity.

"When I came back here, it's true, I wanted to teach you both a lesson. I was still angry at Ethan and hurt and had this stupid, vindictive plan. And I'll admit, it was a very immature one." She looked from one man to the other. "I just wanted you two to feel how I felt. How the girls who you broke the hearts of felt."

She paused, not sure how to continue with what she had to say. In retrospect, she felt silly and childish for even coming up with such a plan.

"But..." Trey prompted. "What now?"

"Look, maybe I don't deserve it and maybe it's very selfish of me, but I want you both. I love you both." She looked down at her hands folded in her lap. "I guess I feel we're good together. Even if it's a little unorthodox, and selfish and all those other things." She graced them both with a hesitant smile. "Sometimes a girl wants the romance novel ending."

"So what do you think, Ethan?"

Ethan sighed and fell back into the sofa, rubbing his chin, which was harbouring a couple days' growth of stubble. "I don't know, I think she's going to have to make it up to us."

Ivy crinkled her nose up at Ethan. "Make it up to you?"

"Yeah," Trey agreed. "Definitely needs to do something to show us she's really sincere." He grabbed the remote and turned the movie off. A soft, sultry melody began to play as he switched to one of the music stations.

Her brow furrowed as she looked from one handsome face to the other. "I don't understand."

The guys exchanged a look and grinned. "We want a striptease," Ethan supplied.

"And not one of those half-assed ones either. I mean strip club quality."

"Are you two serious?" She felt her face begin to warm at the thought of being sexy for them. Teasing was one thing, but actually putting on some sort of stripper show? "That's what you guys want?"

"Yeah, we're guys." Ethan jerked his chin in the direction of the staircase. "Now be a good girl, get yourself all ready and then come down here and show us how sorry you really are."

Taking a deep breath in, she slowly released it and nodded. "All right."

Trey

It felt like an eternity had passed before Trey heard the soft click-clack of her heels on the wooden staircase coming back downstairs. He'd already pulled the coffee table out of the way and replaced it with a kitchen chair – he was nice like that.

They could have spent the evening and well into the next few days arguing back and forth, trying to make reason out of the what's and whys, but as Ethan and Trey waited for her to return to them they'd agreed the best thing to do was put it all behind them and start over. They'd all made mistakes, it was best to move on.

"So, is this acceptable?"

Trey turned to see her dressed in a cute little schoolgirl type of outfit – right down to a ponytail tied high on her head, red and black plaid mini-skirt, to the white blouse that hugged her breasts and cute little plaid tie that matched her skirt. His cock immediately went on the alert and he shifted on the sofa to relieve the tightening in his pants.

He whistled. "You're making me think you had this planned all along."

She laughed. "Does it matter?"

He shook his head. "No, not really."

"Little sister has really grown up." She scowled at Ethan for his comment, which only caused a bark of laughter to come from both men. "Sorry, forget I wasn't allowed to use the sister term."

"That is kinda hot in a fucked-up sort of way, man. Really is."

Her eyes shifted to the chair, sitting in the middle of the living room waiting for her. "Thought of everything, huh?"

"We're firefighters, we're always prepared." Ethan offered.

The buttons of her blouse strained against her chest as she closed her eyes, took a deep breath in and slowly released it, reopening her stunning green eyes and fixating her stare on Trey, then slowly shifting it to Ethan. He could see the fear and apprehension was fading and her confidence building. She walked into the living room, her hips swaying seductively with each step until she got to the chair.

Ivy

She grabbed the back of the chair for support, she was scared – so damned scared. Both men were watching her so intently it was both arousing and intimidating. As much as she tried she still wasn't the type of girl to flaunt herself; deep down she still carried the insecurities. She closed her eyes once more, giving herself a quick pep talk.

When she reopened her eyes, she was surprised to see Ethan standing before her. He touched the side of her face, tracing her lower lip with his thumb. He removed his thumb and lowered his lips to hers. "I love you, Ivy. We do. If you're not comfortable then you don't have to do this."

"Ethan —" It was nice that Ethan was the one who went to her. Trey was very forthcoming with his feelings, however, Ethan was the one harder to read even though she knew him better than virtually everyone. Truth was, he was the one she was worried she'd hurt most.

He pulled back slightly to look deep into her eyes and gave her a reassuring smile. "But I think you can do this…"

She stepped into him, wrapping her arms around his waist and placing her cheek on his shoulder. "Thank you." She looked up just as he lowered his lips to hers. He pulled her tighter as he nipped at her lower lip, his erection rapidly growing against her stomach.

"Hey, hey, hey you two! There's plenty of time for that after," Trey complained from his spot on the sofa. "I've got a rock hard erection waiting to be teased."

Pulling back from Ethan, Ivy looked around his shoulder and smiled over at Trey. "Part of the experience is the anticipation, you know."

"I'm getting blue balls over here, babes, and I'm still slightly uncomfortable with jacking off watching you two make out."

"As opposed to being part of the action?" Ethan asked, cocking a brow up at his friend.

"Exactly. So sit your ass down so she can do her thing."

Ivy redirected her gaze to meet Ethan's. "It's fine. Go sit down."

"All right." He gave her a quick, reassuring hug and kiss on the temple before resuming his seat on the opposite end of the sofa as Trey.

After taking a moment to get into the rhythm of the music, she began to move, allowing the song – a soft, sultry R&B melody – to dictate how she moved. Turning the chair so the back was facing the guys she sat down her legs over each side and gently gyrated to the music – catching first Trey's stare and then Ethan's.

Their stares sent a rush of desire through her, increasing her confidence. Standing, her legs still spread on either side of the chair, she began to unbutton her blouse to display the black lace bra underneath. Backing from the chair she made her way over to Trey first, shedding her blouse and tossing it to the floor as she straddled his lap and began to move against him, her mound teasing his cock through their layers of clothing.

"Umm. That's more like it, baby," he groaned, desire flaring up in his eyes as he grabbed her hips, pulling her tighter to him.

"No touching." She batted his hands away, grabbing his wrists and securing them against the sofa. He could have easily broken her hold, but obliged.

"How's that fair," he asked, chuckling.

"It is." She ran her lips along the side of his neck, nipping his earlobe and continuing to move against his body. Her lips moved along his jawline and just as he attempted to kiss her she pulled back and with a swing of her leg dismounted him, making her way over to Ethan.

"That's a fucking tease!"

She looked over her shoulder at Trey and shot him a wicked grin, followed by a wink. "Isn't that the idea?" Redirecting her attention to Ethan, she unbuttoned the skirt and let it fall to the floor at his feet, displaying a pair of black lace panties to match the bra.

Swinging her leg over his lap she settled onto him, brushing her lips across his. "No touching."

He grinned, lacing his fingers behind his head. "Wouldn't dream of it, Ma'am."

The tempo of the music sped up along with her movements. Grasping his shoulders to steady herself, she ground against his cock, teasing herself as much if not more than him as the rough lace rubbed against her clit each time she rocked against the ridge of his cock.

He groaned softly, hunger filling his eyes as he began to move under her, meeting her movements, dry humping her until she was so worked up she had to get off of him and walk over to Trey before she gave up on the whole striptease and begged them both to fuck her.

When she returned to Trey she scowled at him, seeing he'd undone his pants and had his cock in his hand, slowly stroking himself. "I don't recall saying you could masturbate."

He grinned. "Sorry."

"Liar." Pulling off her bra and tossing it across the room, she settled onto Trey's lap, facing away from him, settling his throbbing member between her legs.

Settling back on him she rested her head on his shoulder and closed her eyes as she began to stroke his cock between her legs. When his hands covered her breasts she didn't demand he remove them, in fact, she relished the feel of his calloused fingers pinching her nipples, turning them into rock hard peaks.

"Mmm, I want to fuck you, baby. I can feel how wet you are through those panties. Let's just end this now and get what we both want."

She moaned softly as waves of need and pleasure washed over her. All she needed to do was pull her wet panties aside and she could slide him into her and take the relief her body was beginning to demand. But not yet.

It took a lot of willpower, but she forced herself from him, leaving his cock dripping with pre-cum. She licked her lips looking down at him, but refused to drop to her knees to take him in her mouth, 'cause if she did it would be over.

Walking over to Ethan she placed a leg onto his shoulder and began to rotate her hips, her lace-covered pussy mere inches from his lips. Grabbing her inner thighs, Ethan pulled her into him and kissed her lace-covered mound, and then pulled the thin strip of wet material aside and exposed her to him. He spread her pussy lips and ran his tongue along her slit.

She cried out, his fingers fisting his hair as she pulled his head tighter to her mound, rubbing herself against his lips. "So much for no touching," he murmured. She attempted to pull away, to remove the lace covering her, but he held her tight and there was a soft ripping sound as her panties were torn away and tossed to the floor.

Her body trembled as her need increased. His tongue and lips were heaven on her as he pulled one wet lip into his mouth, sucking off her juices, and then the second. Ivy looked over her shoulder and caught Trey's stare. He'd stripped completely and was freely stroking himself as he watched the couple.

"Come here, Trey."

She didn't have to ask twice. He stood and walked over to her. As soon as he was within reach she grasped him and began to stroke his length, savouring the sound of his low groan as she stroked him.

Grasping her chin in his hand he tilted her lips up as he leaned down and claimed her lips with his.

Ivy cried out against his lips, as Ethan's tongue thrust into her core, while his thumb and forefinger pinched her throbbing clit. Trey pulled his lips from hers and thrust his cock to her lips. She immediately took him in, swirling her tongue along the head and lapping up the pre-cum.

Giving and receiving pleasure and the building need for release became her only focus. Anything she'd been concerned or worried about, all her upset and anger were gone. Everything melted away and it was just them. It was beautiful, and perfect and so right she couldn't imagine not having them both – it felt like the most natural thing in the world.

"Fuck, I can't wait anymore sweetheart," Ethan said.

She found herself being laid back onto the sofa and Trey pulling his cock from her mouth. Her eyes flew open and she watched as Ethan settled several throw pillows under her bottom, lined his cock up to her entrance and pushed in, groaning loudly as he claimed her. She watched a moment, fascinated by the sight and overtaken with the pleasure of his cock disappearing deep within her and then reappearing gleaming with her juices. The angle was perfect, the head of his cock slamming against her inner wall, stroking her G-spot with each thrust.

"You're not done yet, baby." Her view of Ethan's beautiful, thick cock thrusting into her was blocked as Trey straddled her chest and tapped her lips with his cock.

She slowly lifted her eyes up his stomach and chest, taking in every inch of hard, chiselled muscle until their gazes locked. She parted her lips and he slipped his length into her mouth as she palmed his balls. This time however, she wasn't in control. Ivy closed her eyes as he began fucking her mouth as Ethan fucked her pussy, the two of them using her body for their own pleasure, but bringing her along for the ride. The desire within her was becoming unbearable, she wanted to move against them, with them, but she was secured to the sofa. Her body tensed and she moaned against Trey's cock as her pussy clenched onto Ethan's cock and then her body trembled as she came. Trey's moan echoed hers as the vibrations from her moan sent tremors through him.

"Switch."

What the fuck? She had no idea who said it and she didn't have a chance to even register what was going on, but all of the sudden she was empty and felt alone. She opened her eyes to see Trey and Ethan had switched places. Just as the realization came to her she cried out as Trey's cock slammed into her throbbing pussy with such force that it sent another orgasm through her.

Ivy moaned again, her hands fisting the sofa under her. She attempted to buck against Trey, but Ethan straddling her chest forced her back into total submission, his cock bobbing in front of her mouth. "My turn, sweetie."

She parted her lips and tasted her own juices on him as he slid his shaft between her lips. His cock wasn't as long as Trey's but thicker and he was close to coming, his vigorous thrusts bordering on violent. She palmed his balls, but they were already rock solid.

Wave upon wave of pleasure crashed over her and all she could do was bask in it, but a sudden jolt of pleasure brought her back to reality, as Trey began working her clit as he fucked her. "Come with me, come over my cock, baby."

Oh god, oh god, oh god! The words seemed to repeat over and over in her head as if on a sound loop as the men fucked her without mercy. The pleasure was too much – too intense – and she felt tears fill her eyes.

She would have responded, but couldn't. With one final thrust and low, throaty groan Ethan slammed into her mouth a final time and a burst of his seed filled her mouth. She swallowed his seed as he came, ensuring she got every precious drop of him. His ejaculation sent her over the edge for a third time. She moaned, releasing his depleted cock from her mouth as her pussy clenched around Trey's shaft. Her orgasm was all Trey needed; he slammed into her once more and released muttering, "Oh fuck!" under his breath. A gush of his cream filled her core, mixing with her juices. A second smaller orgasm hit her, but she was too spent to even moan.

She let out a ragged breath, closing her eyes and panting hard as the men removed themselves from her body as she attempted to clear her foggy mind. A soft sigh escaped her lips as she felt someone's lips on hers kissing her softly, followed by his tongue tracing her lips and then withdrawing. Confused, Ivy opened her eyes to see Ethan looking down at her with a peculiar expression on his face.

"Ahhh, I see what he means," he said, looking over at Trey who was naked, sprawled out in an armchair across the room. "So more kiwi you say Trey?"

"Yeah," came the reply.

"What are you talking about?" Ivy turned onto her side and made room for Ethan to stretch out on the sofa next to her.

Ethan laid down and pulled her tight to his side. "Yeah. My semen is salty. Gonna have to work on that. Trey voiced a complaint earlier today and it seems he's right."

What... In the fuck...

She looked over at Trey, who shrugged. "Someone had to tell him." He winked at her. "You're welcome for that by the way."

Ivy opened her mouth to question him further, but stopped herself. "I don't think I have enough energy for this conversation," she murmured more to herself than to her men as she snuggled against Ethan closing her eyes, but Ethan's chuckle told her he'd heard.

"We'll talk later, honey." He brushed his lips against her temple. "I love you, Ivy."

She smiled, but didn't look up. "Love you too… Both of you." She didn't hear a reply as sleep took over.

Epilogue

~ *6 Months Later* ~

Ivy

Ivy squealed as Ethan scooped her up into his arms and walked her over the threshold of the quaint three-bedroom bungalow on the outskirts of Boston that they had just purchased a few days prior. It was a sweet little starter house. The acre lot was nice and private, carefully landscaped with thick, tall hedges on either side of the lot blocking their home from prying eyes of the neighbours.

"This really isn't necessary," Ivy protested, but it was a feeble protest at best, she liked having any excuse to be cuddled next to her man. Not that she really needed an excuse.

"It's tradition."

"Ummm. Right." Ivy frowned when Ethan stopped in the empty living room and deposited her on her feet in the center of the room. "I really can't believe you moved here for me."

"Pay is better and we can keep an eye on you." He gave her a wink, pulling her into his arms.

Ivy grinned. "Like I could handle another man! You two are more than enough."

"I meant school. But, yeah, the man thing too."

She groaned. "You're starting to sound like a nagging wife, you know that, right? Nag, nag, nag." Despite her words a smile formed on her lips. Having him here was having a very positive effect on her grades. With her obsession for revenge a distant memory, her priorities were finally where they should be – her future. Correction – their future.

"Can't help it. You and that medical degree are my meal ticket, baby!" He gave her ass a little slap, making her squeal and fall into his arms. "I can retire and be your full-time love slave."

He was in the process of lowering his lips to hers when the sound of someone clearing his throat – loudly – sounded from behind them. Ethan groaned and lowered his forehead to hers.

"You two realize there's an entire moving van of crap waiting to be unloaded, right?" Trey reminded them, setting a large brown box on the floor in the living room.

Slipping out of Ethan's embrace, Ivy walked across the room to Trey. Lacing her fingers behind his neck she stretched up against him and placed a light kiss on his lips. "We're sorry."

Ivy had originally thought this would be an odd situation to explain to their parents and awkward in general. But they'd all come to an understanding, something they'd decided early on in their relationship. Considering the fact she and Ethan were technically stepsiblings they had decided together to tell their parents she and Trey were a couple, with Ethan living with them. It was just easier for everyone involved to go about it that way. The situation would be re-evaluated if and when the time came for marriage and babies. But for now, it worked and everyone was happy.

"Mmm." He returned the kiss, pulling her flush against him while deepening the kiss. She moaned softly, parting her lips and inviting him in, a rush of heat racing through her, igniting a soft throbbing between her legs.

Ethan

He chuckled watching Ivy and Trey. He'd never seen Trey so enamoured with a woman before. Although, he was sure Trey would say the same thing about him. It took an extraordinary woman to manage two guys, making them both feel like they were both the center of her world – but she was somehow able to do it. However, it did help that the Boston FD had them on alternating schedules so they could both have one-on-one time with her, along with the group time. Surprisingly enough, it worked.

Admittedly, it took him some time – longer than it did Trey – to really embrace the idea. This wasn't the movies, or some novel. It was real life with real emotions involved. Sure, jealousy and the need to compete for her still happened from time to time, but she always managed to defuse the situation and remind them there was no couple, they were a trio – no one more important than anyone else.

Walking over to them Ethan pushed her hair to the side and lowered his lips to her neck, gently nipping at the flesh. Her body trembled and her lips left Trey's as she moaned softly. While it was great to compromise with Trey, sometimes a little healthy competition never hurt. And there wasn't a more enjoyable game than the one they secretly played – unbeknownst to Ivy – on who could make her moan loudest or come first.

Feeling Trey's eyes on him, he looked up and met his friend's gaze.

You're on, motherfucker, Trey mouthed at him, grinning.

The End.

To hear about Terry's new releases and upcoming special and promotions, please sign up for her newsletter. Rest assured we will not spam your inbox.

Newsletter Sign-up

Excerpt from:

What Happens In Vegas... Doesn't Always Stay There

By

Terry Towers

<u>Available Now</u>

Chapter 1

<u>The Present – Genevieve</u>

"Oh, you have got to be kidding me!" Genevieve's emerald green eyes flashed with anger before narrowing as she watched the sexy as sin NYPD officer Dane Porter stroll into her boutique. "What are you doing here?"

A smirk spread across Dane's lips at her question. "You called to report a break-in. I was the lucky one to be assigned to answer the call and take your information."

Genevieve didn't return his smile.

"Maybe I changed my mind." Flashes of her brief tryst with Dane in Las Vegas a couple of weeks prior sprang into her mind. He was a gorgeous man, she'd give him that, with blonde hair that was just a smidge too long to be considered short and rich blue eyes. It upset her that just seeing him standing before her, dressed in his officer's uniform made her remember – and long for – his touch.

Crossing his arms over his thick, muscular chest, he cocked a brow up at her, still amused. "You changed your mind? So, there wasn't a break-in and you're wasting taxpayers' money by making false calls to 911? That's an offense, you realize; I could cuff you and take you in right now."

"Oh, I bet you'd like that, wouldn't you?"

I hate that you've seen me naked! And that I wanted you touching me then... Touching me now... She growled at herself and once again attempted to free herself of her unwelcomed thoughts.

Ignoring her, he reached into the inner pocket of his jacket, produced a pen and pad of paper, then stepped further into the boutique until he was standing before her and began looking around. "What did they take?"

"Fine!" She gave him a little shove as she rushed past him and motioned for him to follow her to the broken glass cases which, up until that morning, held dozens of pre-loved authentic designer handbags. "This way."

She knew she shouldn't act like such a child with him. She was a twenty-five-year-old business owner. She should be acting mature, not behaving like a teenager with a broken heart. But, dammit, she was upset with him and even more upset with herself. She wanted to just forget.

Oh please, he didn't force you into anything. You enjoyed every second of it, a voice at the back of her mind chimed in. Instead of making her see reason, the voice only infuriated her further – because it was right.

"Striking an officer in addition to false 911 calls. You could be in big trouble, Ginny."

"My name's Genevieve."

"You didn't mind me calling you Ginny in Vegas."

She spun around and shot another glare at him. "Very funny. There *was* a break-in." She motioned to the shattered glass of the empty cases. "They took all the handbags. The Birkins, Gucci, Louis Vuitton… They took it all. And they broke the glass of the counter and took all the jewelry and small leather goods. I bet they took well over two hundred thousand in goods."

She felt hot tears threatening to emerge and forced them back. She started with nothing and now much of her most expensive merchandise – three years of gathering and dealing – gone. Sure she was insured, she could rebuild, even if all of her bestselling merchandise was gone, but it would take time. People looking to sell

Birkin bags for below their value for resale didn't come along every day, even in New York.

The amusement faded from his expression as he began to write. "Do you have a list of what was stolen?"

"Yeah, let me check the computer." She made her way into the back office, assuming he'd follow her and not wanting to look him in the eye. If she looked him in the eye she might break down and then look to him for support. She might fall into his arms and the anger she was feeling would dissolve. If the anger was gone then she'd have to admit what they did was what she wanted, regardless of whether she'd admit it to herself or not.

As she sat down at her desk she booted up the computer. She heard his footsteps entering the small office, but didn't bother to look up.

"So they took stuff in the store, but not the computer?"

"My office was locked. They probably had enough without bothering to break down the office door."

"I see. That's possible. You don't have an alarm?"

"Of course I do." Her tone was sharper than intended, but she didn't care. Shrugging, she refused to look up at him. "Guess it didn't work."

"Uh-huh."

She lifted her gaze to lock with his, angered at his dismissive tone. "What? You think I'd just fake a break-in?"

Dane's jaw clenched as he thrust a hand through his hair, all humour lost from his eyes. "Look Ginn- Genevieve, I understand we left things on a very bad note in Vegas, but I'm a cop and I have a job to do. I'm sorry if you were upset with what happened, but I'm trying to be friendly and help you here. Can you please work with me on this?"

Closing her eyes, Genevieve took a moment to steady her nerves, feeling slightly guilty at her reaction upon seeing him again. "I'm sorry. I'm frazzled and seeing you right now, just..."

The tension drained from him. "It's fine. I'll go check out the security system and see if I can figure out why the break-in didn't set it off, while you make me a list of stolen items."

She couldn't help but admire his broad shoulders and back as he turned and exited her office. A mix of emotions raced through her seeing him again. Of the millions of people living in New York and the hundreds of cops what were the chances of her ever seeing Dane Porter again?

The remainder of the afternoon went by quickly. After Dane left she spent the afternoon and into the early evening cleaning up, dealing with the insurance company and calling all of her clients, hoping that they would have items they were willing to sell. She still had a store full of gowns and clothing from all the top designers, but the bestselling items were handbags, wallets and smaller items; the items that were stolen. Apparently, the thieves knew what was easiest to peddle as well. It sickened her that her precious Birkin bags might be sold on a street corner alongside dozens of cheap knockoffs.

Exhausted physically, mentally and emotionally she closed and locked her office door and made her way toward the front of the store. Halfway to the store entrance she heard the bell ring, signalling a customer. Apparently they hadn't seen the closed sign and she'd forgotten to lock the door.

Dammit!

"I'm sorry we're –" Her eyes focused on the person entering the shop and she could have sworn her heart stopped for a fraction of a second.

You have got to be shitting me, as if this day couldn't have gotten any worse!

Squaring her shoulders she glared at the person whose body was framed in the store entrance. "What are you doing here?"

Three Weeks Ago – Genevieve

"I'm sorry Genevieve, but I just can't go through with it," Alex Cane stated, looking more uncomfortable than Genevieve had ever seen him – though she supposed breaking up with her on their wedding day, while she stood before him in her wedding dress would make anyone uncomfortable. Even her slick, rising-star defense attorney fiancé wasn't immune to the shame of the heinous way he was breaking up with her.

"Is there someone else?"

He shook his head, but she saw it in his eyes. There was.

"We've been together since high school, Ginny. Since we were seventeen."

"Exactly, eight years, Alex!" She wasn't sure what she felt more upset by, humiliation or anger. The emotions switched up every few seconds, but currently, it was anger winning out, causing her body to vibrate with the emotions.

He stepped forward and grasped her upper arms in his hands, but she stepped away from him, batting his hands away. She didn't want him near her, or touching her. Never again.

"It's better this happen now than getting a divorce in a year's time."

"So you chose our wedding day to decide this!"

"I wanted to make sure."

She shook her head. "You selfish asshole. How dare you!"

He sighed, taking a step back from her. "I'm sorry. I can… I'll go down and tell the guests the wedding is off."

Genevieve's emerald green eyes widened in alarm. *Oh my God, the guests! Everyone is downstairs. Waiting.*

"Don't do me any favours!" she spat, venom in her tone. "Allow me." The anger within her increased as she pushed past him with so much force he stumbled backward a step, and out the door. She raced down the hallway and down the stairs heading toward the chapel, Alex in hot pursuit.

"Ginny, hold on. Wait!"

At the bottom of the staircase he caught up with her, grasping her arm and stopping her from proceeding into the chapel. "Let go of me Alex, or I swear to God!" Her hands fisted at her sides. She wanted to hit something… she wanted to hit him! But she didn't. She didn't want this day turning into more of a fiasco than it already was.

Seeing the rage in her eyes, Alex released her, allowing her to continue to the chapel. "I can do this," he protested from behind her. He was following, but at a safe distance.

She ignored him. She'd tell everyone herself. Knowing Alex, the weasel that he was, he'd somehow make it sound like breaking off the wedding was her idea. She refused to take any blame for this.

"Everybody," she called out to the half-full church. Not everyone had arrived yet, but there were close to two hundred of the three hundred guests invited already seated and mingling.

Every head turned toward her, their eyes questioning.

"Everyone. I have an announcement to make." She made her way to the altar and turned to face the crowd. The priest for the ceremony looked up from his notes, his brow furrowed, but said nothing. Their friends and family, all waiting, all shocked to see her in her wedding dress standing in front of them before the ceremony.

Alex lingered at the back, keeping his eyes averted. Coward.

"Everyone. Alex has informed me that after eight years together, he no longer wants to be with me." Gasps and murmurs erupted within the church. "Apparently he wants to explore other possibilities and has just recently made this decision. And I guess our wedding day felt like the right time to inform me." The crowd's stares shifted from her to Alex, and back to her.

She was humiliated, but at the same time, she wanted him to feel part of this humiliation and by the redness in his face as he sulked at the back of the church, she was certain he got a small part of what he deserved.

Alex's mother leapt from her seat and she hurried over to her son; his father followed behind. A look of shame and disappointment was evident in both their expressions.

She looked to her own parents and her older brother. She could see her parents were still trying to digest the information, but her brother Brian had already processed it and by the look of fury in his dark eyes as he stood and began to make his way down the aisle toward Alex, she knew what he intended to do. He and Alex had been friends up until that moment, but Genevieve was his baby sister and he was nothing if not protective.

A part of her wanted to see Alex hurting, like she hurt, but not like this. Her wedding had already become a circus; she didn't want it to turn into a brawl in addition. Kicking off her shoes she raced barefoot down the aisle in pursuit of Brian, but she wasn't quick enough. Brian grabbed her former fiancé by the front of the shirt, pushed him against the wall and slammed his fist into the other man's jaw.

Brian's hand pulled back a second time and his fist again made contact. Alex slumped against the wall, his knees buckling under him. Brian was about to hit him a third time when Genevieve grabbed his arm, stopping him.

"Don't Brian. Please."

Brian looked over his shoulder and caught her gaze, indecision filling his eyes.

"He's not worth it. Just take me home. Please." Genevieve held her breath, waiting.

Brian looked back at Alex, hesitated, and after what felt like an endless second released him. "Fine."

They both looked down at Alex, his nose and lip bleeding, cowering on the floor. His mother had begun fussing over him, but when she looked up and her eyes locked with Genevieve's there was only sympathy. Alex had such a wonderful family, they'd welcomed her into the fold and treated her as if she were their own. She was going to miss them and she was sure they would feel the same. She and Alex had been and *should* be perfect together; this made no sense. But it was.

"He's not worth it anyhow," Brian growled, placing an arm around her waist and ushering her away

"No, Brian, he's not."

Once they were out of ear and eyeshot of the onlookers, Brian stopped and pulled a handkerchief from his suit jacket pocket and passed it to her. "For what it's worth, you make a stunning bride, little sis."

Accepting the handkerchief, she took a deep breath in, and slowly released it, fighting back tears. *No he's not worth it,* she told herself. *He doesn't deserve my tears.* However, despite her efforts to keep back the tears, they had a mind of their own as they began to flow down her cheeks, smearing her perfectly applied make-up along their trails. All she wanted to do was go home, get out of the blasted dress and try to forget Alex Cane ever existed.

Chapter 2

Two Weeks Ago – Genevieve

Genevieve looked around as she entered the honeymoon suite. She was in Las Vegas a week after she was stood up on her wedding day. As it turned out, the hotel was prepaid and the price was non-refundable. They'd gotten an awesome deal with the non-refundable pre-purchase of the suite; it hadn't even crossed her mind there would be a reason to cancel when she booked it. The honeymoon had been scheduled a week after the wedding to take advantage of the awesome deal Alex had snagged them. So the choice was either go to Vegas and make use of the room or waste the fifteen thousand it cost to spend the week there. So she hopped the plane – alone – and now here she was.

"Thank you," she gave the bellhop a ten dollar bill as he placed her two suitcases inside the door of the room.

"Thank you ma'am." He gave her a friendly, sexy smile and pocketed the bill. "Would there be anything else I can assist you with?"

Genevieve look a moment to look the handsome Latino man over. He was very good-looking and oozed charisma. He was one of those men who you spent a wild night of passion with and went home completely satisfied never to see or talk to again.

A part of her wished she was the kind of girl that did things like that. In truth, she didn't know what kind of girl she was without Alex in her life. Alex had been her first love and partner. Her *only* love and partner when it came right down to it.

Would he be better in bed then Alex? Her sex life with Alex was okay, not mind-blowing like what she read in erotica and romance novels, but she doubted sex was that explosive in real life anyhow. But as she continued to look at the bellhop she found herself interested in finding out.

"Ma'am?"

She gave her head a shake at her foolish ideas and gave him a tight smile. "That's all. Thank you."

"If you need anything, you know where to find me."

She watched him leave and then went about inspecting the room. Champagne was sitting on the table in the kitchen, chilling on ice. As she wandered into the bedroom, she found rose petals scattered over the bedspread and a bouquet of roses and box of chocolates sitting next to it. She picked up the flowers, brought them up to her nose and inhaled deeply, taking in the sweet scent.

Her mind drifted back to the bellhop. Would it be so bad for her to indulge in a night with someone? God knows, it had been suggested to her by numerous friends before she left. But no. She wanted a connection with someone, needed a connection. Could sex even be satisfying without that loving bond established beforehand?

She huffed, disgusted at herself. *Yeah, 'cause that worked out so well with Alex.* Maybe her friends had it right. No strings attached – just sex – taking pleasure in the strength and heat of a beautiful man you barely knew.

If only I were that type of girl...

Placing the flowers back next to the bed she went over to her suitcases and began rummaging through her clothing until she came to a beautiful, cream coloured Gucci dress. Stripping off her jeans and t-shirt she proceeded to change, slipping into the dress and spending the next half an hour primping until everything from her accessories to her make-up was perfect.

Once done she walked over to the mirror and examined herself. Her straight, black hair fell to the small of her back. It had a glossy shine that most women envied. She was about twenty-five pounds overweight, but it was in all the right places, giving her soft feminine curves. Her emerald green eyes were accented with rich black cat-eye make-up. She looked good, sexy. But instead of making her feel good, it only made her feel more confused. If Alex didn't want her because of the way she looked then what was it? What about her made him not want to be with her? She shook her head, grimacing; she hadn't a clue.

With a sigh, she gathered her golden Chanel double-flap handbag, stuffed her wallet and casino vouchers in it and exited the room. The casino gave her five hundred in casino money as part of the honeymoon package, so she figured she might as well use it while she decided on her next course of action.

~ *Dane* ~

Between poker hands, Dane Porter watched the raven-haired woman as she played the slot machines across from him. He'd been winning until she showed up, however, now he was losing virtually every hand. Disgusted with himself for allowing the vixen to distract him, he decided to give the cards a rest – for now.

His dick was taking over his mind and there wasn't much he could do about it – except find a way to satisfy the urge she was provoking within him. And what better way than introducing himself?

Walking over to her, he leaned over her shoulder. "Anyone sitting here?" he motioned toward the seat next to her.

She paused with her hand on the lever, about to pull down and spin the wheels. She looked from the vacant chair to him. Releasing the lever she spun her swivel chair around to face him, nibbling on her lower lip as her eyes did a more thorough inspection of him.

Not quite expecting her to be so brazen, Dane found himself slightly uncomfortable. "…But if it's taken…"

A smile formed on her lips, amusement in her stunning green eyes. "Is that what constitutes a pick-up line around here?"

He clucked his tongue off of the roof of his mouth and shrugged. "Not sure, I'm vacationing here from New York." He extended his hand to her. "Dane Porter."

Her face brightened at the mention of New York. "That so? I'm also from New York. What are the chances?"

He winked as he sat down next to her. "I think it's destiny."

She rolled her eyes at him. "Okay, that was just cheesy. I expect more from a New Yorker, you're disappointing me."

"Oh, come on! Give a guy a break here. I'm trying to get to know you." He shot another smile her way. Usually women swooned when he turned on the charm. It was evident she was going to be a little harder, but there was nothing he liked more than a little challenge.

Her expression softened. "I apologize." She extended her hand to him. "I'm Genevieve Fennel."

"Genevieve? What a beautiful name."

"You can call me Ginny."

"Staying here at the hotel?" He popped his member card into the machine, slipped in a fifty-dollar bill and waited for the credits displayed on the reader.

"I am. You?"

"I am. A suite on the top floor." He pulled the lever and the wheels began to spin. "So what brings you to Vegas?"

She shrugged. "I'm on my honeymoon."

He froze for a moment. Well, shit. His smile fell. He was really hoping she'd be available. He cleared his throat and pulled the lever again. "Well, congratulations."

"No need. It's a solo honeymoon."

His brow furrowed, confused. Solo honeymoon? He turned his attention back to her. "I don't follow." His eyes lowered to her left hand where a wedding ring should be, but her finger was barren of said ring and he noticed a faint white mark where a ring used to be.

"I was stood up at the altar and the reservations were non-refundable. Being that you're also staying in the suites you can imagine the amount of money that would go to waste if I didn't come." She shrugged, her smile turning rueful. "So here I am."

Dane was struck speechless for a moment. What do you say to a newly jilted bride-to-be? "I'm sorry to hear that." Yup, that was the best he could come up with.

She laughed softly. "Don't be. You had nothing to do with it. It was for the best."

"Were you with him long?"

"Eight years. High school sweethearts."

"Oh, ouch." He turned back to the slot machine, focusing on that a moment as he tried to decide on the best course of action. Stay and try to score, or let her go. It was a tough one.

He watched her out of the corner of his eye as they played, listing the pros and cons in his head. Pro, she was fucking hot. Stunning. And the ache in his groin was becoming a nuisance. Con, she's fresh out of a relationship. She could be vulnerable and maybe a little too needy for a one-nighter at this point. She was young, he guessed early twenties. If she was with her former fiancé for eight years she may have only ever been with one man so she was virtually a virgin.

Dane clucked his tongue off the roof of his mouth. Was her being inexperienced a con? Nope, nope it wasn't. He switched that over to the pros list.

"What, is there something in my teeth or something?"

"Huh?" He was so engrossed in his mental list-making that he'd stopped playing completely and discovered he was staring at her.

"You're staring. I won't lie. It's kinda creepy." Despite her words, there was a twinkle in her eyes and a smile on her perfectly painted lips.

He could feel himself flushing. He wasn't one to get embarrassed easily, but being caught ogling her did it. Maybe because she didn't appear like the average girl he would go for. Looking at her, he could tell she had class. Everything from her poise, to her clothing and how perfectly made up she was screamed it. Nope, she wasn't the typical club hooch he had a tendency to gravitate to.

"Your ex must have been an idiot." He didn't mean to say the words, but seeing her smile widen and her cheeks turn an alluring shade of pink made him glad he did.

"Wanna hear something crazy?"

"Sure, I love crazy."

"He's a lawyer and it was with one of his co-workers. Cliché, huh?"

"Very. And the fact he's a lawyer just confirms my opinion that he's a douche."

"Not a fan of lawyers, huh?" She'd lost all interest in the machine in front of her and her complete attention was on him – just how he liked it.

"I'm a cop; it's in our nature to hate lawyers."

"He was a defense lawyer."

Dane groaned loudly, making a show out of his mock displeasure, pleased to see her giggling at his antics. "Those are the worst kinds. He did ya a solid."

The dark-haired beauty laughed. "You think?"

"I know."

Contact Information

Website: www.elixaeverett.com

Email: terry towers@hotmail.ca

Facebook: Terry Towers

Twitter: TerryTowersXXX

Works By Terry Towers

(Not all books/collections will be available at all retailers)

<u>Available Now - Singles</u>

Frat Party Partner Swap

Hers To Command

Daddy's Special Christmas Gift *(Also Known as His Special Christmas Gift)*

All For Daddy (Taboo Edition)

The Marine's Naughty Sister (Taboo Edition)

Little Virgin Sister's Webcam Show *(Also known as Desperately Seeking A Co-Star)*

Doing Her For Dad (Taboo Edition)

Her Brother, Her Hero *(Also known as Her Marine, Her Hero)*

Her 'What if' Guy (Pursued By The Billionaire)

The Inheritance: Anything He Craves

The Game Of Love: House of Sex, Scandal and Sexy Singles

Moan For Big Brother *(Also known as Breaking The Rules)*

Moan For Daddy

Milk Money

Bought And Paid For

Seduced While She Sleeps

Seducing Big Brother *(Also known as The Seduction Plan)*

An Heir For The Billionaire

Taming A Dark Heart

Behind The Mask

Tamed By The Cowboy

What Happens In Vegas... Doesn't Always Stay There

Trust

The Instructor

Melting Point

Secrets

Seeking Prince Charming

Available Now - Themed Singles

Taken By The Team (Humiliation And Gangbang Fantasies Fulfilled)

Taken By The Marines (Humiliation, Gangbang And Cuckold Fantasies Fulfilled)

The Cop And The Girl From The Coffee Shop

The Politician And The Girl From The Coffee Shop

The Assassin And The Girl From The Coffee Shop

The Bounty Hunter And The Girl From The Coffee Shop

The Firefighter And The Girl From The Coffee Shop

The CEO And The Girl From The Coffee Shop

The Porn Star And The Girl From The Coffee Shop

The Rock Star and the Girl From the Coffee Shop

The Rock Star and the Girl From the Coffee Shop 2: Under Pressure

The CEO and the Girl From the Coffee Shop 2: The Pleasure In Surrender

Available Now - Series

Deceiving Him (The Billionaires' BDSM Sex Club)

Surrendering To Him (The Billionaires' BDSM Sex Club 2)

Hitching A Ride

Hitching A Ride 2: To Trust A Con

Conjugal Visits

Conjugal Visits 2: New Beginnings

Sibling Rivalry *(Also Known As The Rivalry)*

Sibling Rivalry 2: Never Say Never

Sibling Rivalry 3: In It Together

Moan For Uncle *(Also known as Moan For Him)*

Moan For Uncle 2: Keeping It Secret

Moan For Uncle 3: No More Secrets

Moan For Uncle 4: Skeletons In The Closet

Moan For Uncle 5: Love Or Duty

Moan For Uncle 6: To Love And Honour

Moan For Hubby (Moan For Uncle 7)

Available Now - Mirror Editions

(Please note Mirror Editions are mainstream non-PI editions of some of Terry's bestselling taboo works.)

Doing Her For The Boss *(Rewrite of Doing Her For Dad)*

The Marine's Naughty Sister *(Rewrite of The Marine's Naughty Neighbour)*

The Virgin's Webcam Show *(Rewrite of Little Virgin Sister's Webcam Show)*

Seducing Blake *(Rewrite of All For Daddy)*

Now Available - Boxed Sets

Men In Uniform Boxed Set

The Rivalry Boxed Set (Books 1-3)

Crossing the Line Boxed Set

Alpha Male Romance Boxed Set

Behind Closed Doors Boxed Set

The Terry Towers' Taboo Collection Vol. 1

The Terry Towers' Taboo Collection Vol. 2

Naughty But Nice Mirror Edition Collection

The Moan For Him (Moan For Him/Uncle books 1-6)

The Sibling Rivalry Bundle (Books 1-3)

Terry Towers & Friends Multi-Author Boxed Sets

His To Control Boxed Set

Red Hot & Taboo Boxed Set

Our Little Secret Boxed Set

Forbidden & Taboo Boxed Set

Coming Soon

The CEO and the Girl From the Coffee Shop: The Pleasure in Surrender

The Tattoo Artist And The Girl From The Coffee Shop

Works By Nikki Nexus

Available Now - Singles

Seduction Games

Santa's Brothel

The Confessional: The Naughty Nuns Series

The Fire Eater

Taken By The Team (Humiliation And Gangbang Fantasies Fulfilled)

Taken By The Marines (Humiliation, Gangbang And Cuckold Fantasies Fulfilled)

Made in the USA
Columbia, SC
02 June 2017